Planet of the Rings

Vol. 1

A Novel By

Bernard Bayede

First Impression: 2020

Second Impression: 2021

ISBN: 978-0-620-91906-7

Tel: 076 636 7999

Email: khatidexxii@gmail.com

Bound and Printed by: Amazon KDP

For Juliet,
My Soul Mate

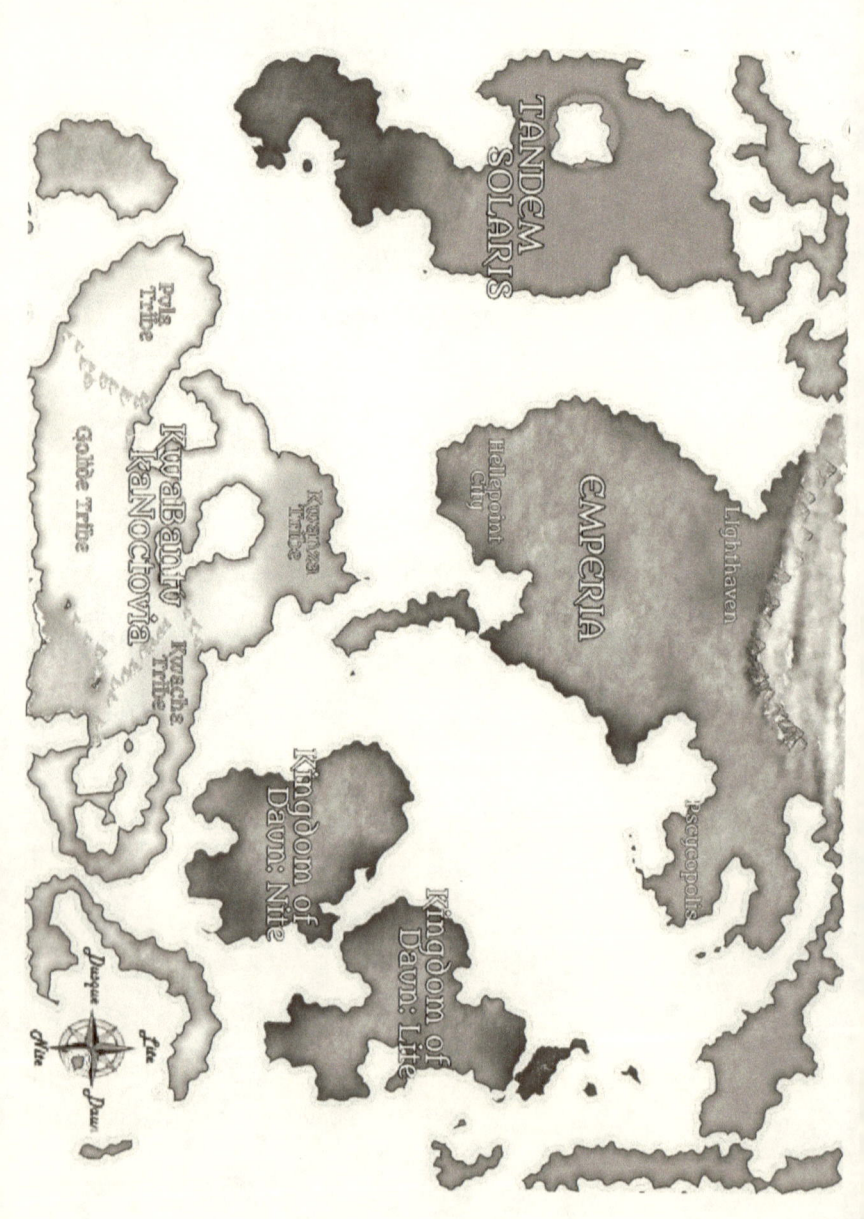

ACKNOWLEDGEMENTS

It's always a strange sensation to complete a book especially when you've been working on it for a while. I think it has to do with that feeling that now that it's complete, you no longer have to work on it. And while there is a sort of sadness to it, it always feels good to have people around you to support you.

I dedicated this book to my wife (who at the point of publishing this book was my fiancée) for two reasons. The first was that it was because of her that I completed this book as from the moment I told her about it, she knew it was the one I needed to publish thus giving me a goal. The second reason was because the last book I dedicated to her, she shared the dedication with the other three most important people in my life.

My sister, Naledi is that person in my life who's always been there, an absolute constant. I guess you could say that's by virtue of being my sister but its more than that. She's also been a good listener whether it was about me going on about my books or me expressing my worries about something to come. She's always been there.

My father, like my sister, has also always been in my life and has been my rock from day one. It's through him that I developed a moral compass and how to give myself a sense of direction.

Then there's my mother who unfortunately, passed away in 2011. To this day it feels like it happened too soon and not a day goes by that I don't remember her. It brings me sadness that she never got to meet Juliet because I know she would have loved her. It was my mother that I attribute my love and passion for writing to as my mother's compassion and understanding for others knew no bounds.

Anyway, I figured I'd give these wonderful people full blown acknowledgements because my last attempt did not do them justice in my eyes and the chances are, with the number of books I plan to write in the future combined with the number of people in my life I have to thank, I won't be writing about them like this for a while.

Hope you enjoy the book.

Contents

A LETTER BY EDDISON RANDALF KESSLER

Mercury 22nd, 492 ADI

To Whom This May Concern,

They say that in the beginning there was only *The Light* and the Darkness. No one knows how they came to be but they have been at war since the beginning of time. It was these two entities that created the six dimensions in their effort to control the universe: their home dimensions of the Heavens and the Underworld; the four dimensions of Fairden, Lloomis, the Ashlands and Limbo where they interacted; and our world, the mortal world, which

1

they agreed to never physically interfere with, only influence.

As a child, I would gaze up at the colorful rings that circled our beautiful world and marvel at how these rings represented the other dimensions and wish more than anything to see them. But as an adult, I know that this shall never come to pass.

For a thousand years this world had known peace under the glow of the *Light*. Ever since the doorway to *Fairden*, the angelic dimension of the arkers, was opened and the prayers of the people were answered by the thousands, the Age of Illumination reigned. From the industrious dynasties of *Emperia* in the *Lite* to the bold clans of the *Bantulands* in the *Nite* and from the fearsome tribes of *Tandem Solaris* in the *Dusque* to the progressive nations of the *Kingdom of Daun*. I know how the legends go. And I know that the universe almost came to an end almost five hundred years ago.

The invasion, they called it. When the dark, mysterious creatures known as daminites rained from the stars in a hail of fire and brimstone. Hellfire they called it, as it wasn't just the daminites that posed a danger to the world but also the manner of their arrival that caused destruction and mayhem.

Warriors from all four corners of the world united in fighting the daminites: wielders in the Lite; drakana in the Daun; warriors in the Nite and horselords in the Dusque. In the end, it was the very air we breathed that did the beasts in. However, no one could have seen the long-lasting damage done by the invasion: the end of the Age of Illumination and beginning of the "age of entitlement". The world was once again divided, with all major kingdoms of the world being ruled by fear of another invasion.

With his deep desire to accrue power, the elected Emperian King commissioned excursions across the nation to look for the special crystals that give wielders their power. After amassing the crystals, Emperia became the leading kingdom of the world with inventors like me at the forefront. It was meant to be the beginning of a time of chivalry and a more civilized age.

First came our ability to generate heat by making use of the blue sparking crystals; then came our ability to heal almost all wounds with the green herbal crystals followed by our ability to communicate across long distances using yellow crystals. With the red crystals giving wielders the ability to move things with only the mind, the construction of towers, bridges, mills and mines was something that could only be described as revolutionary. Unfortunately, with only certain people with the power to use them, these wielders became valuable commodities and treated like property.

These events led directly to their rebellion which resulted in the desperate wielders creating the supernatural species known as

vyrens: immortal, blood-drinking beings –
and their derivatives: wights – undead
beings with no minds of their own except
for one thing: their appetite for human
blood.

These events only escalated with the
creation of bladeslingers by the humans to
meet the growing supernatural threat.
These special humans, imbued with speed,
strength and agility, quickly became the go-
to answer to all supernatural creatures
including the ones that did not originate
from Emperia.

As for me, as an inventor, my experiments
with the supernatural properties of the
crystals were a plenty but none as
significant as the one that led me directly to
my current predicament. Until recently, I'd
never given much thought to prophecies.
They had always been something from the
arkers of Fairden. But through my
experimentation, I'd managed to do
something quite unparalleled: On Saturn

the 12ᵗʰ, 491, I saw the future. And what I saw frightened me.

The world – or rather Emperia more specifically – had evolved far too quickly. Our obsession with being pioneers and using the supernatural to progress the world had robbed the world of its natural evolution. In the future I saw, the world had become obsessed with crystal sciences and would destroy itself. And I knew that I had played a part with my misguided search for enlightenment.

It took my visions to understand where we had gone wrong. After the daminite invasion, we'd lost contact with the arker dimension and as such no longer had our prayers answered. And in our hubris to answer our own prayers, we had played with powers beyond us which would inevitably doom us. It was at this point that I had made my decision.

Having foreseen that my pleas with government would fall on deaf ears, I took it upon myself to resolve the situation and found the means to gather all the stockpiles of crystals I could across Emperia and abscond with them. By Uranus the 22nd, I had all the crystals I could get my hands on and settled my affairs so that by the end of Mercury in the New Year, I would be long gone.

Under the guise of journeying across the world in an epic voyage designed to finally map the unknown places of the world, I will dispose of all the crystals in my possession and then disappear into the night to make sure that they will never be found.

However, with the knowledge of the destruction of the world being so valuable, I have left behind paintings of my visions in various parts of Emperia with the hope that someone worthy may find them and not only save the world from the threats ahead but unite the world not in fear but with hope.

If you're reading this then know that your destiny is already in motion and that fate is set by your own hand.

Yours Hopefully,

Eddison Randalf Kessler.

FORSAKEN
A HELLEPOINT STORY

Hellepoint City: a place of dreams and a place of nightmares. Growing up, Theodora Lange had never really had any love for the place. With its elaborate architecture that consisted of buildings with extremely high ceilings; exuberant number of arches and very wide corridors, Theodora had always found it quite off-putting. Every building looked like a cathedral including King Victor's Palace. It didn't help that the family housekeeper and her nurse always told her scary stories of the monsters that lurked about the city during the night – a tactic designed to keep her from being outside after the sun went down.

However, when Theodora moved away at the age of nine, she'd found herself missing the scary city. It did not help that Theodora grew up to understand that Hellepoint, being the capital of the continental nation of Emperia, was where all the exciting things happened. It was there that the elected King ruled the country with an iron fist. It was there that all the latest in science and engineering was discovered. It was also there where all the docks were that took people to the various parts of the world.

Theodora had been told long ago that there were other places in the world. She remembered how she initially believed the lie that the rest of the world was discovered during the Great Voyage of 492, only to be told much later that the rest of the world was already known by the time Eddison Randalf Kessler pulled off the heist of the century. But since learning that there were continents other than Emperia in the world, she'd wanted more than anything to see them.

Theodora had wanted to see Tandem Solaris in the dusque having heard how half of it was practically a dessert while the other being nothing but jungle having never seen either. She wanted to see Noctovia in the nite which was apparently an ice-ridden landscape with fearsome dark men who had descended from wolves. Then of course there was the Kingdom of Daun which lay in the daun: two massive islands once united but since split by a civil war centuries earlier. Theodora wanted to see them all but knew that she couldn't and that was all because of her father.

Theodora's father, Lord Edmond Lange, was a politician. Having inherited his great ambition of being a ruler from his own father, Lord Edmond had wanted nothing more than to rule Emperia as King. And, like all men and women with even a drop of royal blood in them, Lord Edmond was eligible to be elected King. But after four consecutive terms without being elected and only managing to rise to Vice Count of Hellepoint, the Lord had eventually left Hellepoint, taking a nine-year-old Theodora with him.

This was how Theodora ended up growing up in Lighthaven for the past ten years. And while growing up as the daughter of the Count of Lighthaven had its benefits, Theodora had missed being in the capital and was ecstatic when her Lord father had told her that he had good news: he'd just received word that he was being appointed Count of Hellepoint which automatically made him a part of the House of Dukes – noblemen that answered only to the elected King or Queen of Emperia and were all next in the line of succession in the next election.

"Oh, that's wonderful news, father," said Theodora when she'd heard the news. "So, will we live in the city, perhaps in the castle?" Having grown accustomed to the finer things in life as a Lady, Theodora had always dreamed of living in a castle.

However, her father gave her a solemn look. "Unfortunately, Dora, while that would ordinarily be true as I am a Duke, it's an honorary title and—"

"An honorary title?" said Theodora, worried.

"Yes. Understand, I am, first and foremost, going to be the Count of Hellepoint which means my job will be to run the city of Hellepoint. That means by default, I am in the King's inner circle but in actuality—"

However, Theodora didn't have the patience to listen to how the political hierarchy worked. "Father, where will we live?"

"Why, at the old Lange Manor of course."

Theodora's face dropped. "Oh." While she didn't have a problem with the old manor house – a lovely place in its own right with it being a huge building surrounded by a vast amount of land – it was half a day's horse-ride from the city. Her father had noticed her face.

"Now, now, Theodora. I will have you know there is some good news. Do you remember Oswald Wright and his sister Ember?"

"Yes." Theodora remembered them perfectly. The Wrights had been left to look after the old manor when they'd left. The elder Wright, Oswald and Ember's

13

father had been the groundkeeper when they still lived there. When the Langes moved to Lighthaven, Lord Edmond had decided to allow Mr. Wright to farm the lands and turn it into a plantation. This had turned into a very lucrative business and made Mr. Wright something of a rich man.

He'd eventually opened up three other large plantations in the outskirts of Hellepoint and turned Lange Manor back into a home worthy of a Lord just in time to be named a Lord in his own right. While he'd died before he could enjoy the title, his son Oswald now enjoyed the spoils of lordship which mainly amounted to a respect his family had never afforded before.

Lord Edmond continued. "Well Oswald, or Lord Oswald now, has asked me for your hand in marriage and I have graciously accepted."

"Oh." Theodora knew better than to react negatively. Before she died, her mother had told her that one day her father would arrange a marriage for her and that she had to trust that he would never marry her off to someone untoward. However, Lord Edmond sensed the reservation regardless.

"Now Theodora, you should know that I did not take this match up lightly. In fact, the only reason I felt any inclination to accept the proposal was because of your history as childhood friends."

Lord Edmond had a point. When the Lange family moved into the manor house after her mother had died, little Oz and Ember had become her friends. While others thought it strange that a Vice Count's daughter was friends with the children of the groundskeeper and housekeeper, Theodora had never cared and neither had the Wright children. In fact, her and Ember had become the best of friends and it would have been the same with Oswald if he wasn't always helping his father with chores now and then. They had all three been sad when she and her father had to leave them behind.

Remembering their history, Theodora put on her best smile. "Well, the match sounds delightful father. When do we leave for Hellepoint?"

*

With her undying love for travelling, Theodora had been delighted to hear that they'd be travelling back to the capital by ship. While it was only from one side of Emperia to the other, it was still thrilling to watch Lighthaven disappear in the distance behind them and have Hellepoint rise from the fog ahead of them. Seeing the skyline of towers, castles and four-storey buildings come into view was thrilling.

Ever inquisitive about sailing, Theodora had asked one of the sailors about everything she could about traversing the seas. The sailor had first told her about the four points on the compass: lite, nite, dusque and daun. He'd then told her about how if one wanted to travel to the Kingdom of Daun, one would have to depart from the daun side of Hellepoint City while if one was going to Tandem Solaris, one would leave from the dusque port of Hellepoint which was where they were coming in now.

When the sailor said that only members of His Majesty's Royal Navy were allowed to travel to other nations, Theodora had enthusiastically asked if he'd been in any battles. It was at that point that Theodora doubted the man's ability to tell the truth.

"Battles on the waters have been far and few between; mainly disputes between trade federations for trade routes. Those are often settled by gentlemen, sitting over pipes and alcohol in elegant rooms. No, the greatest threats of the four seas are the mermaids."

"There's no such thing."

"Really? So, you can believe in wielders and arkers and daminites, but you can't believe in mermaids?"

"Well wielders are real enough, sure. Otherwise, how does one use a crystal? Without wielders, there would be no civilization. No running water, no bridges, no elevators. We'd literally be living in the dark if there weren't blue crystals and wielders to

17

make them spark. As for arkers, they all died off during 'The Fall'. The daminites are well documented in all the history books so I can believe in *them*. But mermaids, this is the first I've heard of mermaids, except in bedtime stories, of course."

"And where do you think those stories come from? Legends passed down from generation to generation. Every country has legends, and every legend has some truth to it." The sailor pointed dusque. "From the tandemites of Tandem Solaris: beasts made by reanimating dead daminite carcasses I hear," he said before pointing daun, in the opposite direction. "To the dragons of the Kingdom of Daun."

"Dragons *don't* exist."

"Not anymore but they used to, long ago before the world belonged to man. They died out before our time but there are scientists who have found bones that could only belong to them. That's how the drakana have their dragon-breath."

"No, no," said Theodora, denouncing the sailor's history. "Their dragon-breath comes them drinking potions made from the lava they harvest from the volcanos over there." Theodora remembered learning about this from her tutor just a few years ago. She'd learnt all about the legendary sword-wielding soldiers who answered only to their King. She remembered being fascinated by how their rulers passed their rules down from father to son, giving no other relatives chances to rule.

The sailor had finally heard enough of her doubt. "Fine don't believe me. But don't say I didn't warn you if one day you find yourself in the middle of the ocean and your ship is attacked by beautiful women with fins for feet."

"Hey Cabin-boy," said another much older sailor. "You're not scaring our guests with your tales of mermaids again, are you?"

"It's not a tale if it's true," said the Cabin-boy to the older sailor who by the look of his much cleaner navy-blue uniform was a lieutenant.

The Lieutenant smiled. "It doesn't matter if the stories are true. If Lady Theodora is never going to traverse the seas, then she need not worry of the legends of the sea. What she best be worried about are the legends of the land. Specifically, those of Hellepoint City." This time it was the Lieutenant that pointed, to the city which was even closer.

"And what legends are those?"

"Have you ever heard of a vyren?" The Lieutenant continued when Theodora shook her hand. "A vyren is a human being that's brought back from the dead and feasts on the blood of the living. They're venomous creatures that can only be stopped by a dagger to the heart made of human bone but are also weakened by iron. As the legend goes, the first vyren was turned by her wielder lover who couldn't live without his beloved. What he couldn't know was that the powers

20

that brought her back to life made her unable to physically age and she could only remain alive by feeding off the living. To make matters worse, there was a side effect unforeseen by the wielder which allowed the vyren to make more vyrens."

"How does that happen?" asked Theodora, curious.

"If you get bitten by a vyren and drink their blood before dying, you will wake up in your grave, a vyren yourself."

Now Theodora had a thousand questions but only asked one. "Why would a human being drink the blood of a vyren?"

"Perhaps they were forced to; perhaps they wanted to become immortal. Or maybe, they just liked the idea of being able to move like the wind and have the strength of a hundred men. Perhaps they liked the idea of being able to see for miles at the dead of a moonless night or hear someone talking on the other side of a castle. Who knows? What I do know, is that the life of a vyren is a cursed one."

Theodora looked from the Cabin-boy to the Lieutenant and wondered if they knew that they weren't supposed to drink the sea water. She tried to be as polite as possible. "I don't believe in fairy-tales. There are no such things as mermaids," she said to the Cabin-boy, "and there are no such things as vyrens," she said to the Lieutenant. "And wielders are not out there creating dark creatures of the night. They're helping keep this beautiful place we call home together and you should show them the respect that they deserve."

After bidding them good day and returning to the lower decks to her father, Theodora thought on her parting words and realized that they weren't all strictly speaking true. While he'd been forbidden from talking to her about it, her tutor had mentioned something about wielders that suggested that it wasn't all as majestic as the government would have the people believe. He had mentioned that sometimes, wielders can go bad.

He'd talked about how over seven hundred years ago when the daminites invaded and then the arkers fell, the royal government had desperately sought a means of restitution with *The Light* and used crystals with supernatural properties to do so. However, with wielders being the only ones that could harness the power, they were brought into service. And while those that served were said to garner their power from *The Light*, those that weren't were said to garner their power from somewhere else: the Darkness.

Her tutor explained that those that rebelled against what they believed was glorified slavery on the part of the royal government were quietly labelled darkwielders and were allegedly hunted down and killed by the mysterious 'Brotherhood of the Bladeslingers'. While her tutor had surmised that this was all propaganda designed to make the public feel safe and that he'd never even seen a bladeslinger in person, it did make him weary of wielders, wondering if one could turn to the dark at any moment.

Theodora had quietly dismissed all of this. After all, she didn't think of wielders as slaves. Any wielder that she'd ever met had always been gracious and kind and never showed any ill will to her or anyone else. In fact, as a little girl she'd wanted to become a wielder when she grew up. Of course, that had been impossible as one had to be born with the power and the ability to wield it when they were older. But alas, she'd always found the whole mythology interesting.

*

When they arrived at Hellepoint, Theodora was escorted to the carriages. As she made her way through the docks, she couldn't help but take in how disgusting it looked. The wood was a soggy dark brown, almost green from all the sea water that sprayed on it while the business of the place made it look so uncivilized. Then there were the dockworkers, all dressed in dirty brown coats and pants, covered in sweat and dirty sea water.

Theodora suddenly found herself wondering if this was the same town she'd grown up in. "Don't worry dear," said her father. "You will not be staying in a place like this."

"Of course, not father. The thought hadn't even crossed my mind," she lied. Theodora suddenly heard sniggering behind her from one of the workers and shot them a hard look. That's when her eyes landed on *him*. It was his eyes that pulled her in… they were so blue.

While she'd made a point not to look at them except with a glance, she now found herself transfixed by this man. The first thing she noticed was that he didn't fit. He was far younger than the rest with slim muscles and more kempt hair. He was the only one of the lot that didn't laugh. Lord Edmond had noticed her pausing and called out to her to come along.

They got into the horse-drawn carriage and started away. While the carriage took them through the city, Theodora couldn't help but think of the man at the dock, the thought of him sticking to her like glue.

She'd barely managed to shake the thought him out of her head to take in her former home.

To her relief, the city was just like she remembered it, grand and larger than life itself. The buildings made of stone and rock, stood solid, only separated by roads where horses and horse carriages moved with the rhythmic sound of trots. When she looked up, she saw that she couldn't see the sky and remembered that as a child, her only memories of sunny days were over the valley on the outskirts of town, the only place that, if one stood at exactly the right place, one could see glimpses of the rings.

Theodora was thankful when her father said that he needed to make a stop at the House of Dukes. When the carriage came to a stop in the town square, Theodora got excited. While Lord Edmond told her to stay in the carriage, Theodora did no such thing and stepped out to see that they were right outside a beautiful four-storey building with a façade that had an arch at every window. She looked across the town square and her jaw dropped.

26

The town square was in fact a circle and in its centre was a very tall tower with an hourglass at the top. At that exact moment, a large bell located in the middle of the tower – some two hundred feet up – tolled three times which was immediately followed by the giant hourglass flipping between two pillars so that the next hour could begin.

"Wow," she said.

"It's a wielder that's doing it," said an old lady on the side of the street. "You must be new to the city if you're finding that fascinating."

"Actually, I was born here," she told the old lady. "I've only just returned. But it's been ten years which would have made me nine the last time I was here. I don't remember that hourglass turning though."

"That's because it hasn't turned in over two hundred years. Not until the Viscount announced that they'd discovered a red crystal."

Theodora looked at the woman as if for the first time. "A red crystal. That means that wielder is moving the hourglass with their mind."

"Not just the hourglass but the bell too. You can read all about it in there," she said pointing to what looked like a cathedral.

"What's in there?"

"It used to be where people went to pray to *The Light* and waited for the arkers to show up. But that was centuries ago. Now it's a library dedicated to *The Light* and those with the power to wield it."

Theodora wanted nothing more than to go inside but she knew that her father would be back momentarily and thought better of it. She'd come back some other time. But when she did, she wanted to read all about all the new discoveries that were made in her absence.

It took almost an hour to ride through the city before they arrived in Hellepoint Valley. After that, Lange Manor came into view and they were into their family lands. Theodora looked out of the window and saw that the lands were just as beautiful as she remembered. The grass was just as green and the lake on the daun side of the manor house was just as blue. The manor house itself was a masterpiece of a building.

With twelve bedrooms, multiple living rooms and a kitchen that one could get lost in, it was definitely a place for a Lord. When they got to the front door, they were greeted by two smiling faces. Both were red heads, and both were stunning, especially Ember. Gone was the round-faced girl and in her place was a twenty-one-year-old beauty with porcelain white skin and fiery red hair, curled and placed on one side of her face.

Oswald Wright looked devilishly handsome with red hair up to his shoulders, parted to the right with a clean-shaven face and a nice dark red three-piece suit complete with a ruffled necktie and ruffled sleeves showing at the wrists. He was a complete gentleman. When they got to the Wrights, Lord Edmond, a gentleman himself, reintroduced everyone making a point to present her to Oswald.

Oswald took her hand and kissed it. "Lady Theodora, what an honor it is to be graced with your beauty once again."

Theodora blushed. But before she could answer, Ember was suddenly on top of her, arms wrapped tightly around. "Oh Dora, it's good to see you. We're going to be sisters now."

When Ember finally let go, Theodora smiled. "It's Theodora now. And I am so glad. We've always been like sisters so it's only right that we make it official."

Not having the patience to let them talk as women, Oswald gestured inside. "So, shall we?"

As they continued in, Lord Edmond spoke with the now-grown up Lord Oswald. "So, Oswald, I was sorry to hear about your father. He was a good man. I know it's no consolation, but I am glad he died with the respect of a Lord…"

As the Lords spoke, Ember pulled Theodora in another direction and they started heading to another room. "So, Dora, you have to tell me everything. What was it like in Lighthaven? Is it true that you can see the Lite Pole glowing on the horizon at night? They say the sun never goes down over there."

"Please, it's Theodora. Dora makes me sound like little girl. And you can't see the Lite Pole from Lighthaven. As it turns out, the name of the town is just that: a name."

"So, you haven't even seen the Lite Pole?" said a disappointed Ember.

"I didn't say that. Ships don't dock at Lighthaven which means you have to go inland past the mountains that enclose the Lite Pole. But if you stand at just the right place, you can see it."

"See what?" said Ember, now excited.

"The mountain that's so tall that it leads right to the heavens. You can't see the top because of the cloud bank."

31

"And what about the base? Is it true that there is no base and that the mountain is floating on this glowing light?"

"I don't know. We never got close enough to see the base of the mountain. But if that's true, how do you think that's even possible?"

"Oh, come on, Theodora?" she said with a sneaky smile. "It's *The Light* of course. The source of all good in the world. There are many that say every supernatural creature owes a debt to the power of *The Light*."

This gave Theodora a thought. "Even the bad ones?"

Ember made a face. "What bad ones?"

"Darkwielders?"

"Propaganda," said Ember as a matter of fact, a little too easily. "There's no such thing as darkwielders."

"And what about undead supernatural creatures? I was recently told about these creatures called vyrens." Theodora didn't know what to make of the frozen-shocked look on her face. "Have you heard of them?"

"Dora, who told you about vyrens?"

"It's Theodora. And I thought vyrens weren't real so why does it matter?"

"It matters because this city is not what it used to be. There's a storm brewing Theodora, and it's been brewing for a while now. Superstition is in the air and it's taken over the city."

"Superstition? What are you talking about?"

"Rumors of wielders being killed; sightings of phantoms; corpses being found with all their blood missing."

"Blood?" said Theodora, remembering the Lieutenant's story. "Are you saying that vyrens are real?"

"I'm not saying any of this is real. But what I am saying is that this whole city is living in fear. Why do you think that the previous Count didn't run for a second term?"

Is that why father got the position? thought Theodora. Was it because no one else would take the position?

Ember saw the fear in Theodora's eyes. "You're afraid. Good, you should be. And be thankful that we live all the way out here in the Valley, far from the city." Ember then gave her another hug. "It's okay, sister. My brother won't let the things that go bump in the night take you away."

*

It was strange being back at the manor. A week had gone past and Theodora had spent it getting to know the lay of the land once again. Her father had been busy travelling to and from the city, making her fear for his life with every trip he took. She had barely seen Oswald which she thought was strange but instead had

34

spent time with Ember as they passed the time by regaling each other with tales of their time apart.

Having spent every day with Ember, it was strange when after days on end without seeing him, Oswald had appeared and asked her to go for a walk through the grounds. Once again, he was dressed like a gentleman, this time with a silk-woven lampa and matching breeches and his red hair tied up into a ponytail.

"Lady Theodora, I must apologize for being so absent since you arrived. It's just that the farming business is booming and I'm looking to export livestock to the Kingdom of Daun which has kept me busy."

"Wow, the Kingdom of Daun." Suddenly, the part of Theodora that longed for adventure came alive.

"Yes. As it turns out, they know nothing of pork and lamb. I shall be selling pigs and goats to the traders of the Kingdom in exchange for gold crystals."

"I see. And will you be travelling to the Kingdom of Daun?"

Oswald shook his head. "Unfortunately, not. My ambitions lie here with this great city." He saw the look on her face. "Lady Theodora, I feel it's important for me to tell you the truth." They'd come to a stop, so she sensed that this was serious. They were close to the lake now. "Ever since becoming a Lord, I have wanted nothing more than to rule Hellepoint as King."

This confused Theodora. "But you can't, not if you don't have royal blood in you." This got Theodora curious. "Wait, are you of royal blood?" Perhaps he was a secret second or third cousin to one of the current King's children.

"No," said Oswald carefully. "But I don't have to have royal blood in me if I marry someone who does."

It finally dawned on Theodora where Oswald was going with this. "Oh. So, is that why you asked my father for my hand in marriage? It was my royal blood that you wanted?"

36

"Now Theodora, it's not that simple and you know it. We've known each other all our lives and I can now look after you. For one thing, you will never have to set foot into the city ever again. You can stay here and raise our children in peace, at least until your father and I clean up the city."

"You and my father. Does he know why you proposed?"

Oswald shifted as if about to confess another truth. "Your father understands the need for a successor. So, once we are married and I have royal credibility in the eyes of government, I will be your father's second in command in ruling this city as Viscount."

Theodora tried not to react to his way of pronouncing Vice Count as Viscount. It was a thing that only people who were not born to nobility would say. It only set in stone the idea that she was only being used as a tool by a boy who always wanted to rule over the people that had treated him less than. However, what bothered Theodora more than anything else was the idea of being stuck at Lange Manor for the rest of her life and not seeing the rest of the world.

"Would it not be better if I went with you to the city and we lived there so you could—"

Oswald immediately shook his head. "No. Your father made it clear that I could only take your hand in marriage if I kept you away from the city."

"Why?"

"Did my sister not tell you about the city? It's at a tipping point."

"It didn't look like it was at a tipping point when we were there last week at the town square."

"Well, it's mostly after the sun goes down that you see it. But rest assured, there is something to fear and you would do best to stay away. And I will do my best to clean it up, for the sake of our children. So that one day they may rule."

*

After confirming with her father that afternoon that he had in fact made a deal with Oswald, Theodora had questioned the idea of him being superstitious. He'd confirmed that superstition or not, people were dying and in very strange ways. Perhaps that's why he carried his sword everywhere he went.

While almost all conflicts were fought with swords, the world had evolved so far that only military men were seen with them. Regardless, every Lord still had a sword which they'd keep in the house unless sensing a danger. Unlike the crude weapons of the past, swords carried by Emperians had beautiful hilts that continued into a handguard. A Lord's sword was always decorated at the hilt.

Legend had it that the most-rare swords were grafted with melted white crystal, making them indestructible. Theodora was never sure if her father had such a sword. But seeing him carry it around made her understand that the threat was real. Regardless, that did not arrest her desire to journey into the city.

And since she was watched like a hawk during the day, she'd decided to travel there at night.

Foregoing the carriage, Theodora had travelled by horse. The hour went past fast but gave Theodora enough time to figure out exactly where in the city she would go. She'd decided on the only place she knew for sure: the cathedral of *The Light*. When she arrived at the circled square, it was dead quiet which sent a chill down her spine. *Where are all the people?*

She dismounted the horse, tied it up and gingerly approached the giant wooden doors. Unsure if she should knock or simply enter, Theodora pushed the door to find that it was open. It moved with a very audible creek. Inside was a giant space with arches dominating the ceiling and windows. Every corner had a dark shadow with the few candles that were there barely managing to light the place up.

In the room were a series of pews for people to kneel without hurting their knees. It was clear that they were there from when people used them as benches.

However, in front of every pew was a long bench with drawings carved into it. Theodora stepped closer and saw that the carvings actually depicted the history of Emperia. When Theodora considered how many benches there were, she realized that said history could actually cover the events of the whole world.

"Now what is a girl like you doing in a place like this at this time of night."

Theodora turned around to find the man she'd seen at the docks, the one with the ocean blue eyes. He was still dressed terribly but the lack of light made his handsome features more potent. Theodora hadn't heard the door open. "Where did you come from?"

The man pointed to the booth which had two sides. The man had come out of one with the other's wooden door still being closed. "I was sending a message to someone in Pscycopolis."

Theodora understood. The sending of messages across long distances was something achieved by wielders using a split yellow crystal. When two

41

wielders held each crystal twin, then they could communicate with each other telepathically no matter where they were. However, with yellow crystals, like all other crystals being rare these days and thus expensive, it was easier to post a letter.

"How are you able to afford it?"

"My parents were noble. My father was Lord Jacob Dominicolas."

"You're a Lord," said Theodora shocked.

The man shook his head adamantly. "My *father* was a Lord and my mother a Lady. I'm Lucas. No title."

This threw Theodora off. Why would anyone in their right mind throw away the life of a Lord to be, from the looks of things, a peasant? "I've never heard of the Dominicolas name."

"You wouldn't. My parents weren't exactly known for supporting the government, so the name is not exactly something that's spoken amongst nobles."

"Why didn't they support the government?"

"Because they supported the freedom of wielders. They fought for the abolishment of wielders being forced into service."

"I don't understand. What do you mean forced?"

Lucas gave her a haunted smile as if just the idea of what he was about to say was disheartening. He looked around and pointed to the carvings on the paintings. "They say that this place houses the history of *The Light* and where people came to pray back in the day."

"Yes, I was told that but what does that have to do with what you just said about wielders being forced into service."

"Everything. You see, history is written by those with power and influence." He was talking about the House of Dukes and all the Lords of Emperia. "The true history of Emperia is horrifying and begins after the Great Fall of the Arkers. These archives would have you believe that the arkers were destroyed by demons released from the Underworld. They'd have

43

you believe that Emperia and its obsession with the crystals was a result of wanting to protect the country from any further threats be them from the skies above as was the case during the daminite invasion or from the dimension below. But the truth is that the arkers were slaughtered by humans."

At this point Theodora shook her head. "I don't believe that. Arkers had preternatural speed, strength and could heal themselves as well as others. There's no way that humans could pose a threat to them."

"Not unless they were imbued with strength, speed and agility of their own after drinking the lupta prada potion."

Theodora's eyes widened. She knew what he was implying. "Are you saying the arkers were killed by bladeslingers?" She remembered what her tutor had said about bladeslingers and how their abilities came from drinking a special concoction made from a secret potion called lupta prada. But while Theodora barely believed they existed, what little she did believe, she at least believed they were good. They allegedly hunted monsters for Light's sake. "But I thought they only hunted darkwielders and vyrens."

Lucas' eyes opened up with amusement. "I wouldn't take you for a girl who listened to propaganda. Then again, you are walking the streets of Hellepoint in the middle of the night which is oddly ironic now that I think about it."

Theodora scoffed. "Firstly, I'm a woman not a girl. And secondly, just because I've heard all the rumors, it's doesn't mean that I believe them. Take your story for instants."

"You don't believe me?"

"You're a stranger. One that's claiming to be a Lord to boot. I mean, what Lord would dare lower themselves to working at a dock?"

"Well, if you let me finish the story, you'll understand why." There was a silence which Lucas took as permission to continue. "After the slaughter of the arkers, the government immediately made the bladeslingers the official creature hunters of the world. But with the rumors of the slaughter of the arkers by their hands, this was not made news and they operated as quietly as possible. Instead, what the government did broadcast to the nation as news was that wielders would be their new guardians.

"You see, this was always the plan. The reason the government slaughtered the arkers; the reason they installed wielders into prominent positions is because they'd found a way to control wielders and make them obedient. That's why you'll never find a wielder speaking out of place. It's because of fear."

"Fear of what?"

"The bladeslingers. If a wielder steps out of line, they're immediately labelled as darkwielders and hunted down and killed by the edgemen."

"And where did your parents come into this?"

"They believed that wielders should have the choice of whether to serve the King or not and fought for their rights. Then they died in a fire."

That sounded suspicious to Theodora, but she let it go and actually found herself sympathizing with this stranger as she knew what it was like to grow up without a mother. She couldn't imagine growing up without both her parents. "I'm sorry to hear that."

Lucas took a moment before continuing. "Anyway, after they died, I realized that all their hard work didn't really amount to anything as wielders are still in service and darkwielders are killed every day so that Lords and Ladies can live in luxury." These words got Theodora to swallow hard. Thankfully, Lucas continued. "Not wanting the life that's paid for by the blood of glorified slaves, I ran away from it all and have been living a nomad life, hand to mouth."

Theodora, wanting to venture away from the topic of living the life of a Lord, picked up on something. "But wielders aren't slaves. They live just like everyone else does. They go where they want to go; live where they want to live and be with the ones they love."

"Perhaps but they can't do what they want to do, not if what they want to do is not in the service of the government."

Theodora scoffed again. "This is crazy."

Lucas, realizing just how much he'd said, nodded his head. "You're right. Perhaps it's best you forget everything you heard here tonight." When she scoffed again, he shrugged. "I have. I'm not interested in fighting a fight that cannot be won. So instead, I opt to live my life to the fullest."

"And that life involves working on the docks?"

He shook his head. "That's a means to an end. It's more about experiencing all the things I didn't as a Lord starting with the seedy underbelly of this city and ending with finding a way to leave here."

This got Theodora's attention. "Wait, you want to travel the seas? Because that's been a dream of mine since I was a little girl."

Lucas shook his head with a smug smile. "No, I was thinking bigger." He'd lost her. "I want to go to another dimension."

*

Theodora hadn't gotten a chance to speak more to Lucas about what he meant about travelling to another dimension as they were interrupted by her horse being startled by something and becoming ridiculously rowdy. When the two of them had gone outside to check on it, fog began to billow into the circled square. That was when Lucas insisted that she go home and return during the daylight if she insisted on being in the city.

The trip home had somehow taken longer, and Theodora was sure that she was being followed but every time she looked back, there was nothing but treaded road. She arrived at the manor house and stealthily made her way back inside. However, before she could get to her room, she heard voices talking.

"I'm not sure about this, Ember. She's an innocent person. She doesn't deserve to get caught up in this."

"She's not going to get caught up in anything. I thought you made arrangements that she remain here when you come into power."

Theodora recognized the voices. She headed towards them and stopped when she came to a corner. While she couldn't see the Wrights talking, their shadows were cast on a wall she could see with the angle of the candlelight making them appear quite large.

"I did. But she spoke of staying with me in the city and with the way she ran off tonight, I don't think that there's any way of keeping her from Hellepoint."

"Fine, then let her come with you then and suffer like the rest of them." Oswald must have given Ember a look. "What, do you expect me to care? She's a Lady, Oz with royal blood in her for that matter. Those people have looked down on us for centuries. When you get into power and level the playing field, they'll finally feel what it's like to be us."

"You forget that we're noble too now, Ember. Won't the very people we're fighting for rebel against us?"

"We've discussed all this, Oz. As long as they see us bringing down all those snot-nosed Lords, they'll rally behind us. Behind *you*." A door suddenly opened and both shadows jumped. "Quick, someone's coming. So, just stick with the plan and everything will be alright." The candle was blown out and they were gone.

Theodora didn't know what to make of what she'd just heard. *Are they plotting to overthrow all the nobles? To what end?* This night was just turning into one big night of revelations, particularly what it meant to be a Lord. Did the rest of the world think that poorly of them? Was that the reason that Lucas had turned his back on all of it?

All of this had gotten Theodora into thinking. In fact, she hadn't gone to sleep with so much on her mind. All she could think about was what it was like to live a life without the power of nobles. She needed to find out. But with her not knowing where she would start, she realized that there was only one person she could trust to assist her.

While she'd tried to go earlier, in an attempt to heed Lucas' advice, Theodora had only managed to sneak out in the late afternoon. She needed to find him and find out how he was doing it. She made her way to the docks, once again on horseback. However, by the time she got there, it was night out and the place looked abandoned. She was about to leave when she heard the howling of wind coming from the ocean. While she initially made nothing of it, fear began to creep through her when she saw fog starting towards her.

Knowing better than to find out what was going on, Theodora turned her horse around only to be suddenly pulled off of it. When she looked up, she saw three men surrounding her. They didn't say anything as she pleaded for her life. But the begging fell on deaf ears. That was when she kicked one in the groin and began running away but only got a few feet before they caught up. They were about to start ripping her clothes off when another man came out of nowhere and began beating them up.

Making good use of his fists and legs, the man successfully managed to knock one out and send the other two on their way. That's when he came into view and she saw that it was Lucas. "Need a hand?" He lifted her off the ground.

"Lucas. Thank the Light you were here." That's when she wondered. "What are you doing here?"

"What are *you* doing here? I thought I told you to only be in the city during daylight."

"Well, I was looking for you actually."

"What for?" Lucas spoke the words as he led them away from the docks and into town with her horse in tow.

"Well, I'm looking for a tour guide of sorts."

"Excuse me?"

"Into the underbelly of the city." When he gave her a confused look, she continued. "I want to know what it's like to live outside of nobility."

Lucas laughed. "No, you do not."

Theodora furrowed her brow. "Yes, I do," she said, not liking being told what she does and does not like.

"Why? You live a comfortable life, why would you want to tread the gutters of this city."

"Why do you?"

"I told you why."

"No, you told me you wanted to leave the world. But you didn't explain why you needed to tour the gutters first."

"I need something first. Now answer my question." Lucas listened as she explained what she heard last night. "Well good for him thinking he can change this world and take it from the nobles. I, for one, think it's a futile mission and want out."

"And to get out you need what exactly? You didn't say."

Lucas thought for a moment, almost fascinated by her tenacity. "I'll tell you what. I'll tell you when I find it."

Theodora's eyebrows lightened. "So, we have an accord?" She'd stopped so he could shake her hand.

He took it and then proceeded to kiss it. "If only you knew what you were in for." While she was already flustered from the kiss, his smug smile almost melted her. She'd never felt this way in the presence of a man.

*

As the weeks went by, sneaking out of the manor house had become a routine. Since Oswald and Ember were aware, she'd had to convince them that she'd only snuck out to the grounds and to the lake. While they claimed to understand, she didn't know if the lie had been effective. Regardless, that was her story, and she was sticking to it.

In reality, she'd meet up with Lucas at the edge of the valley and they'd proceed with their night-time adventures. Those adventures had started off innocent enough with them going to a tavern seemingly exclusively used for drinking alcohol. They very quickly graduated to an illegal card game where Lucas showed surprising proficiency. He'd explained that he'd been taught the skill of gambling while he still lived as a Lord and when she asked what he did with the gold crystals, he claimed to use it to support himself. But Theodora suspected that this wasn't the whole truth.

As their adventures continued, with underground fist fights and then sword fights, Theodora began to pick up on how whenever Lucas won any gold crystals, he'd always speak to someone and give them a couple of crystals. When Lucas decided to change things up and take her to a secret establishment where they sat down and watched a man dressed in Solari garb perform a musical instrument, Theodora decided to ask Lucas about it.

"So why are you always giving your gold crystals away every time you win them?"

"What do you mean?" he said, deciding to play the fool with her.

"Lucas, I see you every time, talking to someone and giving them a crystal when the conversation is over."

Lucas smiled. "Perhaps I'm procuring something."

"What?"

"If I told you it was jewelry for you, will that end this investigation?"

Theodora was stuck for words. While she believed that she'd hidden it well, the truth was that Theodora had found herself falling for Lucas. She'd dismissed it as just a crush and since he'd never brought it up once and she was betrothed to another man, there had been no point in announcing it. But now here he was, telling her that he was buying her jewelry.

"Were you buying me jewelry?"

This time it was Lucas who looked flustered. "Did you want me to buy you something?" He recovered his confidence quickly. "It's just, you're engaged to marry Lord Oswald, so I figured you didn't need the romantic aggravation."

Theodora took a second to recover and effectively re-established the status quo. "Oh, you're quite right. Engagements are to be respected and after all, this is a business arrangement of a sort. But I can't help but notice that you didn't answer my question. Who are these people you keep talking to and what are you buying from them?"

Lucas, eager to assist in forgetting their previous conversation, confessed. "Information. I'm buying information from them."

"Is this about that item you spoke of needing for your journey?"

He nodded.

"What is it?"

Clearly not wanting to speak about it in front of anyone else, Lucas stood up and gestured for her to follow. It was only once they were outside that Lucas explained. "Theodora, what do you know about dimension gateways?"

Theodora thought for a moment to the lessons she received where philosophy blended into the sciences. "I know that scientists call them chromaholes."

He nodded. "But what do you know of opening them?" He continued when he saw that she was lost. "Well, from what I could gather, opening a gateway or chromahole requires a power source which serves the same function as a key and something else to hold the door open. The information I've managed to gather has helped me piece the information together and basically you need a combination of crystals and a wielder to use them."

"And have you gotten these crystals and a wielder?"

"It's not that simple. Those crystals have to be used in a specific order and each has to be in a specific phase for this to work: powder, dust, liquid. This means I also need someone who's studied spellcraft to help me. The latest information I've received was where I can find him which means by the end of the week, I could be gone."

"End of the week?" Theodora hadn't meant to sound so shocked or disappointment but there was no hiding it now. "Lucas, you can't tell me that this is the last week we'll see each other."

"I'm afraid it is." He saw the look in her eye. "Theodora, I can't stay here."

"Why not? Why do you have to leave me?" Theodora immediately regretted her words. "I mean, why do you have to go?"

"It's complicated."

"Well which dimension do you want to go to?"

Lucas sighed, realizing that he was going to have to explain himself. "Well, I wanted to go up to the
60

Heavens to try and somehow bring my parents back here. But then I realized that this world is a terrible place to come back to so instead I'm going to go to Fairden to see if all the arkers really are dead. Because if there's even one still left alive, I'm going to bring him back and get him to save this wretched place and make it how my parents would want it."

Theodora couldn't believe what she was hearing. "Lucas, your plan is crazy. And you don't even know if they're any arkers alive. This could be a place you can't come back from."

"If I don't find what I'm looking for then there's nothing worth coming back to and I might as well stay in Fairden."

"Nothing to come back to?" Theodora was now upset. "Am I not worth returning to?"

"That's not what I meant. Theodora, I don't want to leave you behind, but I can't take you with me. At least for you, there's some semblance of a good life you could live here. Me, I don't belong here."

"How can you say that? Lucas, you're a good man."

Lucas shook his head. "No, I'm not. Theodora, I didn't tell you this before, but I was against what my parents were doing, what they were saying. I was like you. I believed that the life of a wielder wasn't so bad that they needed to be saved. I... *I* killed my parents. Not on purpose of course. I didn't know that my parents were in the fire when I started it, but I lit that fire to try and warn them to stop and now they're dead. And I'm stuck here having to go through life knowing that everything they stood for was right. So, I have to go to Fairden and find a way to correct this. And if the place is abandoned, then so be it. It shall be my prison." A tear fell from Lucas' eye. "I have to go."

"No, Lucas wait."

"Theodora, I have to."

"And I'm coming with you." She paused to let the shock ware in for him as much as for her. "I didn't realize until just this minute that I'm in love with you. I've never met a man with such strength and

62

compassion, and I can't imagine my life without you. It's like I've known you my whole life."

"What about the man you *have* known your whole life? Are you prepared to leave him and the life he can provide for you?"

"There are only two things I have ever wanted since I can remember: to travel to places I've never seen before and to share that with someone. You're the only one who can give me both."

Lucas wasn't sure what to say but he was sure that he knew what he wanted. "Then it's settled: tomorrow night, we leave for Fairden."

Tomorrow? "What happened to end of the week?"

Lucas smiled, lighting up her world. "The only reason I was going to stay that long was to spend more time with you before I left."

It was in that moment that her heart melted. There was no denying it: she was in love with him. The Lady in her had been too polite to admit it but it was true. She wondered if that had been the case the moment

63

their eyes had met for the first time out by the docks, but it didn't matter because that was the case now. And now it was time to make the preparations.

*

When Theodora got back to the manor house, she was expecting it to be the usual routine of her simply sneaking in and going straight to bed. But this time, sitting there in the chair in her room was Oswald. "My Lady, we need to talk." He was sitting in the dark, making him to appear like a silhouette of himself. "I know what you've been doing, and it needs to stop. In the name of your nobility."

Theodora wanted to laugh. "In the name of my nobility? Oswald, I know all about how much you despise Lords and Ladies. I heard you talking with Ember and I know that you're planning of stripping us of our titles anyhow so why do you care about my nobility all of a sudden."

"Because it's not that simple. It's never been that simple." Oswald then displayed his point by lighting the candle next to him except that he didn't do it with a match. Instead, he'd struck a blue candle against the table and lit the candle. As the crystal touched the candle, a small spark emitted proving what he was.

"You're a wielder," she said, finally coming to the realization.

"We both are," said Ember stepping out of a shadow like a ghost stepping out of the world. "We have been all our lives."

This confused Theodora. "That can't be. If you were wielders, then the King's men would have come to collect you. He would have brought you into service."

"And our mother never allowed that to happen," said Ember explaining. "She married our father to hide our identities and forced us to grow up in some kind of poverty just so that we wouldn't be discovered."

"Why would she do that," said Theodora, "when she could have allowed the government to bring you into service and take care of you. They would have paid for your schooling and given you a proper life."

Ember scoffed. "Poor, naive, rich girl who doesn't understand how the world works. Dora, in this world wielders are either slaves or fugitives. This paradise that you've created in your mind doesn't exist."

Theodora didn't like Ember's tone which included her calling her by that name. In fact, Ember should have been calling her Lady Theodora, but this was not important right now. What was important was what they were planning, and she had a feeling they were just about to get to that point.

"At least it won't until we make it so." It was Oswald who explained rather than Ember. "When I rise to Count, replacing your father I'm going to make subtle changes to the constitution but not enough to stop me from rising all the way to King. And once I am King, I will be able to abolish the law that says that all wielders must serve the throne or else face punishment. No, by then, Lords and Ladies will be facing punishment!"

"But in order to do that," added Ember, "my brother needs to marry a woman with royal blood in her." Ember was now speaking with a menace in her words. "He needs to marry you and he can't do that if you run away with that gutter rat."

"Lucas is no gutter rat. And I am leaving with him. And *if* we come back from where we're going, we'll be bringing change to this world. But not that kind of change."

It was clear that they didn't understand what she meant, but judging from the look in Ember's eye, she didn't care. "So, I take it you're saying that you will be leaving then?"

Theodora was barely finished nodding when Ember lifted her hand as if to choke her, except she was choking the air between them, However, Theodora was stunned when she began to feel her throat close and couldn't breathe. It was only then that she noticed something red in Ember's other hand. It was a red crystal which explained how she was able to choke her with her mind.

"How does it feel to be a Lady now, *Dora!*"

"Ember, calm down. We need her alive, remember?"

"Doesn't mean I can't have some fun first."

Oswald was about to warn her sister again when another voice spoke from behind her. "Let her go, *now!*" Ember barely reacted to Lord Edmond's presence in the room until he raised his sword. "I said, let her go."

Ember let Theodora go but didn't lose the smug look on her face that she'd been wearing since revealing her power. "And what do we have there? A sword? Lord Edmond, look at the size of the crystal I have." Indeed, it was the size of a small boulder. "I could bend that blade like a twig in a second."

"Perhaps," said Lord Edmond. "Except this blade is covered in melted white crystal which, as wielders, you should know makes this steel nigh indestructible. But if you care to try then go ahead." Neither of them moved. He turned to Theodora. "Theodora be a good girl and get up and get behind me. We're leaving."

The Wrights watched as Theodora did as she was told. It was Oswald who spoke first. "I'm afraid we can't let you leave," he said calmly.

"Oh, you'll have to kill me to stop me."

"Well, that's no problem," said Ember. "It's her we need alive."

"Dora RUN!" said her father just as her metal trunk came flying across the room at his head. Lord Edmond swung his sword at it and it cut right through the chest like it was nothing. It turned out that he wasn't bluffing about the sword and the white crystal. But Dora didn't have time to admire her father's swordsmanship.

Theodora ran for the door and left the manor house before sprinting as fast as she could for her horse and taking off down the street. As she galloped away, she wondered if her father was still alive. She cried at the thought for losing him. But there was no going back for her. In fact, with the way things were, there was no staying behind for her. Now Lucas was her only salvation.

*

Theodora remembered Lucas telling her where he stayed: in a basement in a building on the edge of the city. She also remembered him telling her never to come there but she had no choice. When she got there, she knocked on his door until he answered with a worried look on her face. He told her to come in.

She told him everything including how she thought for sure her father was dead. "They're wielders Lucas. There's no way he's still alive."

"Well, we have to go back," he said.

"No," said Theodora. "I can't go back there. Lucas, we need to leave tonight. Take me with you, there's nothing left here for me anymore. And I—"

Lucas silenced her with a kiss. It was a thing of beauty, majestic in every way. Just the taste of his lips was something special. And it was almost tragic when he finally pulled away. "I will take you with me but not before I check on your father and make sure he's alright." Lucas, who'd been shirtless, revealing to her just how muscular he was, put on a white shirt and his dirty brown coat. "Wait here while I go. Where is your horse? I'll need to borrow it to go up to the Valley."

"It's just outside, at the edge of the alley." She stepped outside just to show him the horse but waited as he went down the alley and to the horse. It was then that Theodora noticed the fog which hadn't been there when she arrived. While she'd never truly gotten her head around what it was, she had deduced that there was always some kind of danger around the corner when it appeared. She was about to call out to Lucas when she heard a voice speaking to Lucas, just out of view.

"Sir, I would like a minute of your time."

Theodora recognized the voice. It was Oz. "Lucas, NO!" but it was too late. Oswald must have been choking him with his mind because she saw Lucas double over in pain with his hand around his throat. Acting fast, Theodora ran down the alley and just as Oswald came into view, jumped on him.

While Ember, who was also there, pulled her off Oswald and subdued her, her distraction proved to have worked as Oswald had dropped the red crystal and thus lost his power. Lucas did not waste time and started throwing punches. When Ember saw that Oswald was losing this fist fight to a far more experienced Lucas, she tried to grab for the red crystal only for Theodora to kick it away.

"No," said Ember, scrambling for the red gem, "no, no no!" When she finally got a hold of it, she turned around to see Lucas now behind Oswald, choking him out or even trying to break his neck. It was at this point that Ember lost control of her temper. "NOOO!!!"

Unbeknown to her, Ember had channeled her anger into the crystal, and it manifested as energy and anything not nailed down on the street was suddenly thrown through the air with such force that she cleared the street. Windows shattered from the impact and Ember's eyes flared with craze. She held out her hand, gesturing at Lucas who began to choke again. When he let go of Oswald, in her fit of rage, Ember twisted her wrist and Lucas' neck broke.

For a moment, it felt like time froze until Theodora saw Lucas crumble to the floor in a heap and she screamed. "NO!!! Lucas!" She ran over to his body and fell over it. Meanwhile, Ember attended to her brother who looked at her, completely horrified.

"Ember, what have you done?"

Ember seemed to understand the accusation. "I had to do something. I had to save your life."

"That's not what I mean. Ember, all that power," he said solemnly, "you can only channel that much with dar—"

She nodded almost crying. "I know. Only darkwielders can use that much power."

Oswald looked at the devastated Theodora and then to her sister. "There's no escaping it now, Ember. They'll know that there was a darkwielder here and they won't stop searching. Not unless someone takes responsibility." Ember began to cry until Oswald continued. "That's why I'm going to stay here and let them arrest me."

Ember's eyes bulged. "What? Oswald, *no*. you can't take the fall for this." But Oswald wasn't going to hear any of it and began pushing her away. "Oz, no. They'll hang you."

He didn't care. "GO!" When Ember was gone and the bell started ringing, Oswald turned to Theodora. "Dora, I'm so sorry."

"Get away from me!" she screeched as he tried to console her. "Your sister killed the man I love."

Oswald spoke steadily. "No, I did that."

"No. I don't care what arrangement you made with that murderer. I know what I saw!"

Oswald then simply lifted the red crystal which he must have taken from Ember. "And they'll know what they see: a man, a wielder with the murder weapon in his hand. Dora, you can say what you want but they won't believe you. They'll believe me."

Theodora looked at him with venomous eyes. "You're a monster!"

"I'll be whatever I have to be to protect my sister."

It didn't take long for the King's soldiers in red coats to arrive. But it wasn't them that handled the arrest but rather another man dressed in a simple black attire that consisted of black trousers; a black coat that ended at his thigh; a black waistcoat over the only thing that wasn't black: a white shirt with no ruffles. His look was completed with black spurred boots, black leather gloves and a big black hat. When he pulled part of his coat back to reveal a large iron knife on a holster on his hip, Theodora knew immediately what he was.

"My name is Brother Samson. I'm going to have to ask you to put the red crystal on the ground and take a step back. If you refuse, I will bury this here blade dead in your heart, you hear?"

Instead of immediately complying, Oswald's hatred of the prejudice against wielders was brought to the surface. "Brother?" He laughed to himself. "I can't even warrant an Elder coming out here to arrest me? Where's your master?"

"You're familiar with the structure of the Brotherhood, I see. Then perhaps this does need to get violent. And if you're so familiar with our ways, then you'll know only 'Learner' are accompanied by a *mentor*," he said correcting him. "Now, will you come quietly?"

Oswald made him think about it before dropping the crystal and putting his hands up. The bladeslinger gestured for the red coats to take Oswald into custody and then approached the devastated Theodora and knelt next to her. "Hello Miss—"

"Lady," said Theodora correcting him. "It's Lady Lange."

"Lady Lange, I'm sorry you had to go through this, but I wanted you to know that your friend here will receive justice."

"No justice will be enough."

"You might find yourself reconsidering that when you realize just how many people will be saved once the hangman is done with him."

It was at that moment that Theodora realized that there would be no justice at all here. A man that didn't kill her beloved, would die while the woman that did was out there, free. There was no justice here. Lucas had been right about this world. There was nothing for her here and now because Lucas was dead, there was nowhere for her to go.

*

"Your Holiness, after the testimony of the witness," said the man in a plain black gown and white wig pointing at Theodora across the room. "and the

77

evidence presented, it is this court's prerogative to hang this man for the murder of Lord Lucas Dominicolas." The words earned cheers from the crowd in the courtroom.

As the prosecutor continued his closing speech, Theodora watched Oswald who was completely calm standing in the middle of the room. It was clear that he'd accepted his fate however unjust. The prosecution had also included the death of her father which led to Oswald being labelled a darkwielder. If only they knew of the real darkwielder who'd disappeared off the face of the planet.

Theodora was so overcome with rage that she was almost glad that Ember had disappeared because otherwise she might kill her herself. That was when Theodora saw a glimpse of someone in the crowd that made her look twice. But when she looked again, they were gone. She was suddenly interrupted by the smack of a gavel.

"Oswald Wright, you are hereby stripped of the title of 'Lord' and sentenced to hang by the neck until death." Another smack of the gavel. "Court dismissed."

Theodora watched as the red courts made their way to Oswald and then began escorting him away. But before they left the room of now-shouting people, Theodora saw her again, slipping something into Oswald's hand before Oswald was taken out of the room. But Theodora didn't care about him, she cared about her… it was Ember.

Theodora moved as quickly as she could and exited the building to the main street which was packed with people. But Theodora managed to spot the fiery redhead and crossed the street to the building across and went down the alley where she saw Ember disappear into. She was immediately met with the point of a sword.

"Recognize this, dear *Dora*?"

She did. "That's my father's sword. What did you do, take it off his dead body?"

"I'd love to banter with you but I'm on something of a deadline," she said before smiling, "pun intended."

"What's your plan here? You don't actually believe that you're going to rescue your brother before he hangs, do you?"

While Theodora hadn't meant to sound smug about her brother's imminent demise, Ember had certainly taken it that way as she poked the sword in her shoulder. "You know this is all your fault. I hope you do know that."

"It's my fault you and your brother killed the man I love!?" Now Theodora was getting angry.

"You should have just gone with the plan and no one would be dead."

"It is *your* fault that my father is dead. It's your fault that Lucas is dead and it's your fault that your brother is about to die. And I will kill you before you get anywhere near that noose."

Ember pressed the point of the sword into Theodora's shoulder again, anger growing. "Oh, you're going kill me? You're going to kill me, are you? Go ahead and try. Go ahead and try!" Theodora didn't dare. "And I'll have you know that my brother *will* die today but what comes after will haunt this forsaken city for the rest of time."

This threw Theodora. *What in the world is she talking about?* Then she remembered seeing Ember slipping her brother something. "What did you give him?"

"Something that will ensure that he doesn't stay dead."

"Good Light, what did you do?"

"What I gave him, *Dora*, was a vile of vyren venom and a vile of vyren blood." Ember smiled when Theodora's eyes popped open. "You should be proud since you practically gave me the idea."

81

"You're going to turn your brother into an immortal, blood-drinking monster?"

Ember nodded. "And he will raze this city to the ground."

Theodora was too scared to roll her eyes. "So, are you going to kill me now?" No answer. "That's why you cornered me, to kill me?"

"Oh no. When my brother rises tonight, he's going to need someone to feed on. And I'm sorry, but that's you." She pressed the sword into Theodora's shoulder one final time. "Tonight, you die."

*

Theodora had never been a fan of graveyards and this one was no exception. Naturally, it was the dead of night when Ember had dragged Theodora at sword point to the cemetery. The cemetery was just outside the city and didn't hide the fact that it was a random plot that had gone unwanted when the city was built. Strangely yet fittingly, there was a low hanging fog that seemed to be permanently etched in the air, shrouding the whole area. Considering her deduction of what the fog meant, surely there was no doubt of what they'd find.

Unfortunately, as they navigated the cemetery, there was more than one spot with newly disturbed soil and no indication of who had been buried there forcing Ember to guess which one belonged to her brother.

"So, what now?" asked Theodora.

"Now," said Ember throwing her a shovel she'd picked up at the entrance, "you dig."

With no thought given to the dress Theodora was wearing, Theodora began to dig. As she did, she wondered what she was going to do to get out of this situation. Could she hit Ember with the shovel? But even if she tried, all Ember would have to do is swing that sword and it would slice through the shovel like it was nothing. No, she needed a better plan than that.

And what about Oswald and the monster he would be when they uncovered him? Surely, he was the real threat? She needed a way to getting rid of him. That's when her shovel hit something. Ember asked what it was, and Theodora revealed that it was a wooden box the size of a man.

Unable to tell if the box was new or not, Theodora was forced to open it to reveal that it wasn't new at all, Inside was a human body that was maybe a few months old. What was even more disturbing was that the person wasn't alone as the box also had a skeleton underneath it.

Ember was not impressed. "Do you see? Do you see now the indignity we have to suffer even after death? That was a wielder and they buried him in a mass grave. Where's the decency in that?" After a moment, Ember's eyes looked away. "Well, this isn't him so let's move on to the next grave." She pointed away. "Over there."

Unbeknown to Ember, while she'd looked away, Theodora had remembered something and acted quickly. She grabbed a bone from the skeleton the size of a small dagger and hid it in her dress behind her back. It was the Lieutenant's words from her journey into Hellepoint that reminded Theodora of the mythology of vyrens: they could only be killed by a bone dagger to the heart.

Theodora then moved onto the next fresh grave. It was only on their third try that they found the right grave. As soon as they found it and she opened the wooden box, Ember had pushed Theodora aside and jumped down to Oswald, cradling his head as if he'd just died. A moment later, she checked his neck where they'd broken it, a tear falling down her cheek before she moved on to business and checked his mouth. Inside, where they would ordinarily have been canines, were sharp white fangs.

"He's started the transition. He'll awake any moment now."

Theodora wasn't sure why she hadn't started running the moment Ember had jumped down into the grave but when the now-undead Oswald opened his eyes, Theodora had seen enough and bolted from the grave. She could barely make out Ember instructing her dead brother to "feed" but a moment later, Oswald was in front of her, having moved like the wind and his bloodshot eyes had murder in them. While his skin had already looked like porcelain before, it was now almost as white as snow. *No wonder vyrens operated exclusively at night.*

Theodora tried to grab for the bone, but Oswald was too quick and in a split second, his fangs were deep in her neck. While initially shocked by the pain of something sharp biting into her, she was alarmed to find that the venom in the fangs was oddly soothing. Her neck had gone numb as Oswald began to drink her blood. While she could barely feel her blood leaving her, she knew that she'd be dead soon if she didn't act fast.

Struggling with all her might, Theodora pulled out the bone and moved it between them and launched it into his chest. She missed the first few times, so she did it again until Oswald stopped feeding, having felt the new wound in his chest. They parted and she saw the shocked look on Oswald's face which actually had a little bit of life back in it.

Ember saw her brother crumble over the same way that Theodora had seen Lucas fall when he'd been killed and once again shouted "no!" and ran over to him. She immediately knew what had happened seeing the bone dagger sticking out of him and didn't hesitate to plunge Lord Edmond's sword into Theodora's belly, fatally wounding her. As Theodora fell to the ground, slowly dying, Ember attended to her brother who was also dying slowly.

"Oswald? Oz? Oz?"

"Ember," said Oswald. "Ember, I need to say something."

"I'm here brother."

"Ember, you need to stay away from the Darkness. Please, don't become what they want to make people believe you are. Don't become a monster." Oswald then began to bleed from the mouth as he began to expire, still dying slowly.

87

While Ember continued to cry, seeing Oswald's blood gave her an idea and she looked at Theodora to see that she was still dying but not yet dead. Inspired by some evil notion and with revenge in her heart, Ember dragged Oswald over to Theodora and placed his dying body over Theodora's dying body so that Oswald's head was over hers. Ember then pulled out an iron dagger and slit Oswald's throat over the mouth of Theodora letting his blood pour into her!

Theodora immediately understood what was going on and tried to spit the blood out, but Ember pressed her mouth to the wound. "My brother may not want me to become something evil but that doesn't mean I can't damn you for eternity." Ember then pulled her brother off of Theodora and brought the iron dagger to her throat. "Now you're going to spend the rest of your existence without the one *you* love and just maybe, if there is justice in the world, you'll feel just an ounce of what it's like for us." Ember then slit her throat killing her!

*

Theodora had never put much stock in dreams but ever since she started dreaming of Lucas, she was sure they had a meaning. As they walked hand in hand across the green fields of Lighthaven, she wondered how a man she'd only known for a few days had affected her so deeply. Her only regret about her time with Lucas was that it was so short.

While Theodora was well aware that this was a dream as she kissed Lucas under the sunlit sky of Hellepoint where the rings of the world gave off a feint shine on the horizon, she couldn't help but feel that this time was different. For some reason, she felt a sense of finality in this dream, like it was the last she would have. That's when she remembered what happened: she'd died!

Suddenly Theodora wondered if all the stories she'd heard about Hellepoint had been true. The place really was a forsaken city that was perhaps beyond saving. She pondered what had become of her from the moment she arrived and how now that she was dead, was never going to get an opportunity to travel the world. That's when the dream began to slip away, and everything became quiet.

In the dead of quiet, Theodora found herself able to hear everything. *This isn't right. Dead people can't hear things.* She could hear her own heartbeat which was alarmingly fast. But it wasn't just her hearing. She could also smell something, and it was rotting. She could also smell soil and realized that she was still in the graveyard. It took a moment for her to realize that she wasn't truly dead. She was undead!

When Theodora opened her eyes, she initially found herself unable to see until her eyes quickly adjusted to the darkness and she saw that she was in a coffin. When she initially tried to push it open, she realized that she'd been buried. When she tried again with all her might, she was shocked by her own preternatural strength as she burst right through to the surface.

Looking around, she could tell that she was still in the graveyard, but Ember was long gone. She looked up to see that the sun was setting, and she realized that she'd been dead throughout the day however the fog of the night still hung low. She then turned to the sight of the city before looking towards the ocean, far in the horizon. She pondered her choices. She knew that she was now a vyren and she also knew that Hellepoint already had enough problems as the wretched hive that it was.

While she knew that this was a curse, she also knew that she had preternatural powers which meant that she could now travel, and no one was going to stop her. Now there was no need to return to Hellepoint. That's when she felt a feeling in her gut: hunger. No… she was *thirsty*. She knew right then that she wouldn't be travelling the world. Taking a moment to understand her new reality in her forsaken nature, she started for the city, taking note of how the fog followed her as she made her way to her new haunt.

TEN

DECADES

LATER

THE STORY OF
THE METAMORPHER

When Sando Golide woke up, it was to the sight of his sister, Phala, who was smiling. This was unusual as he normally only saw Phala at the feasting hut where their morning meals were served. He wondered what was going on and why she was smiling at him.

Phala had a smile that could light up a room. There was something about the way her facial expression just worked on her face; her dark brown skin curling with into neat creases. It was no wonder that she had the eye of every young man in the tribe. Of course, it helped that she was the daughter of the King of the Golide tribe.

"Have you got something in your teeth, Phala?" said Sando in his native Bantu tongue. "What are you doing?"

Phala rolled her eyes at Sando's well-nurtured sense of humor. "Wake up brother. The council has gathered. I think they're about to decide on your request."

Sando bolted upright. "They have? Have they said anything?"

"You know that you'd be the first to know. Now come, brother let's eat. I have a good feeling about today."

Sando got up and put on his heavy fur clothes, including his boots and gloves. All were made from the hide of musk ox and were dark brown, almost black. They were worn out from all the time spent outside in high contrast to the furs worn by the women of the tribes which were light brown and groomed to look beautiful.

They exited the room to a sight that Sando enjoyed every day: the beautiful view of their tribe spread across a wide valley. The lands they lived on, once simply called the Bantulands but now called KwaBantu kaNoctovia were ice-ridden and perpetually cold with snowstorms being a regular occurrence but not without their charms, especially when the clear blue sky allowed the sun to shine down on the land and the people to see the five colored rings that shot across the horizon. In the distance, Sando could just make out the tower that stood between the two mountains that separated the Golide tribe from the Kwanza tribe up lite.

"Wow," said Phala. "Who I wouldn't kill for this view."

Sando looked at her and rolled his eyes. "If only you were being poetic." They began to walk. "So, who will you be fighting with today, sister?"

"No one. Contrary to what you may believe, I don't fight all the time."

"Oh please," said Sando remembering all the way back to when Phala was ten and insisted on joining the other young boys in learning spear fighting. In the eight years that had past, Phala had never lost the taste for it. That was probably why she'd triggered the curse – something very rare for a woman of the tribe to do in this day and age – and why she'd managed to do it at the age of fourteen.

Phala defended herself. "It's true. I listened to father when he told us that fighting isn't the solution to all our problems."

Sando remembered that lesson and how their father had also regaled them of the tale of how the four tribes of the Bantu people had found peace back in the day and formed a treaty that didn't see them kill each other over one tribe member being on another tribe's land. "Diplomacy ends more wars than spears," he'd say. Of course, with Sando having the warrior blood of the

Golide royal family in his veins, it was a lesson he'd found hard to learn himself, often also finding himself in plenty of duels as well.

As they continued making their way down, Phala continued to muse her jealousy of the view. Their village had gone through quite the evolution in the past three centuries going all the way back to what the foreigners called the Great Voyage of 492. That was when they arrived, bringing with them their language, their sciences and their greed. While it was the gold crystals the foreigners wanted from them, they ended up taking something far more dangerous when they trekked to a forbidden part of the Bantulands. However, by the time they were banished from what they arrogantly tried to rename 'Noctovia', they'd taught the Bantu people about building, mining and milling and thus the evolution of their village.

It was a small town now, in truth as the Golide tribe had begun to build their huts upwards as well as outwards, using wood hardened with rare melted white crystal to make their foundations indestructible and erecting the dwellings atop each other. While the tribe was reluctant to build any higher than three stories, they made exceptions when building onto hills. As such, the huts built on hills were much higher up than even the two-storey huts built at the base of the valley. As a son of the King, Sando had been afforded one of the highest built huts in the village. But since he wasn't the oldest of the King's two sons, he didn't have the highest hut. That belonged to his older brother and heir to the tribal throne, Daba Golide.

As they made their way away from the sleeping huts and further into the village, passing the kitchens where breakfast was being cooked and the blacksmiths where weapons were being maintained and tools were being made to mine, Phala looked at him curiously.

"So, you never told me why you want to do this?" Phala looked at him, gaging his expression. "Why do you want to go out there?"

"Well why did our ancestors do it?"

"Those were different times, Sando. That was before our people had work to do that actively make us productive."

"Wow," said Sando. "Spoken like someone who has no respect of the old ways."

"I do respect them, Sando. I just recognize old being the important word in that saying. Besides, we haven't truly forgotten anything our ancestors have taught us. We've just improved on them."

Sando wondered if his sister had a point. Was he really suggesting that it would be better to sleep in tents and huts built of straw and clay rather than reinforced wood and fight with weapons inferior to the foreigners? Was he really saying that it was better to get sick and die from a lack of green herbal crystals than to trade with foreigners for medicine? Granted, the Golide tribe still didn't trade with foreigners, wanting nothing to do with them and instead traded with the Kwanza tribe who in turn traded with the foreigners, but it was still something their ancestors would never do. Was he saying that was better?

Phala continued. "Besides brother, if you really want to live like our ancestors did, you could always join the Kwacha tribe."

Sando laughed. "And be boring and superstitious. I'd rather join the Pula tribe."

This time Phala laughed. "And become a religious oaf. I think not. Besides, could you imagine yourself with no hair wearing their white furs?"

Phala looked at him as if wondering what he'd look like if he cut his shoulder-length dreadlocks and swapped his musk ox skins for polar bear skins. She wondered how they would clash with his dark brown complexion in contrast to how his current furs complimented it. And what would they do to show his tremendously muscular physique?

"No, I think you're better off here with us. And at least we are not as far gone as the Kwanza tribe," she said, making one final plea in her defense of their modernization.

Sando nodded in agreement with that one. Apart from their willingness to trade their mined gold crystals with the foreigners from Emperia for medicine and exotic food, they had also adopted the foreigners taste for their strange clothing which included a lot of colors. However, the Kwanza did live much more lite than them meaning it was slightly less cold with snowstorms being far and few between. Of course, their case was helped by their willingness to trade with the other three tribes.

"I can't help but notice that you didn't answer my question though," said Phala. "Why do you want to go so desperately? You'd be the first in a generation to do this."

Sando was surprised that she didn't understand already. "It's because it's the last opportunity that I'll have to trigger the curse. When I turn eighteen in Jupiter, I will no longer be able to, like you and Daba."

Phala gave him a melancholy look. "This is what this is all about? Oh Sando, I don't think this is something to look forward to. They call it a curse for a reason."

"You and Daba don't seem to see it as a curse."

"That's because we don't speak about it. But the lack of control when the change happens and the pain we go through," she said, her expression changing slightly, "it's unimaginable."

"Yet the whole tribe treats it as an honor."

"You're the son of the king, Sando. You already have an honor."

Sando shook his head softly, not wanting to be harsh. "I'm the second son of the King. All I am to this tribe is a safety net. I need an honor that's all my own and this is the only way I know to get that."

Phala finally understood as they continued on to the feasting tent where most of the tribe was already gathered and eating. Sando and Phala headed to the royal table where their mother sat waiting. When they asked her where Daba was, she told him that he was attending King's business in their father's stead since he was with the council deliberating on Sando's request.

The feasting hut was a giant room held up by reinforced wood with a roof made of straw. Like almost all the huts, the walls were made of a combination of clay and stone while the roof was made of dried stalks on wooden trusses. It was a generally warm place thanks to the hot food served inside, brought in by the tribe members allocated to the kitchens. They brought the cooked food in large black iron pots after cooking them on open fires outside.

While the stews and steam bread were usually left for supper as they were the best to eat when it was colder, a creamy white porridge was usually made for breakfast made from maize imported from the Kingdom of Daun. Over the years, the tribe stewards had become inventive with some of the imported food and stiffened the porridge into sadza also eaten with meat or stew.

Sando had polished his plate just in time to be greeted by an elder. Sando recognized him as one of the tribesmen that sat on the council. "Your father, the King would like to see you."

Sando was suddenly nervous but hid it from his family the only way he knew how. "You do know I'm aware he's the King, right?" he said standing up. When the elder just gave him a blank look, Sando instantly regretted it. "Sorry," he said as they began walking out of the hut, "I just start making jokes when I'm nervous."

"Hmm," said the elder. "Then I would have expected you to be the village jester by now because you should be a nervous wreck considering what's about to happen."

"Thanks," said Sando, finding his humor again. "Thanks for that. You're really inspiring courage there, Baba." It was a sign of respect to call all elders and council members by 'father'.

"Enough jokes," he said as they approached the Council Hut. "Let's go inside so you can learn your fate."

The circular hut was smaller than the feasting hut but since it only needed to house twelve men, there was no need for it to be bigger. While it was structured like the other huts, instead of beds like the sleeping huts or tables and chairs like the feasting hut, the Council Hut consisted of benches that formed something of a circle around the inner perimeter with a bigger chair directly opposite the door. On the chair was Sando's father, King Impi.

King Impi Golide was a man in his late fifties yet still in impressive shape with his build towering over the other councilors. Wrapped in similar clothes as Sando, a key difference in their appearance was that his dark brown skin was a little more wrinkled and his dreadlocks a lot longer. He wore a stern look on his face.

By Bernard Bayede

Sando remembered his royal courtesies and bowed. "Inkosi."

Impi gestured to a small bench in the middle of the room. "Please my son, sit." Sando did as he was told. "Before we give our verdict on your request, there is one thing that we need to discuss as men."

"What would that be, father?"

"Your reasons. Why do you want to be the first Golide to take a spirit walk in three generations?"

What was with everyone and asking this question? Sando knew better than to hide the truth from his father and the King. Although he was sure he knew the reason. "It's my intention to trigger the curse and become a meqa-moya like my siblings," he said before politely gesturing to Impi himself, "and my father before me."

The look the King gave Sando showed that he already knew this as the reason. "But why, my son? Explain to me why becoming meqa-moya is so important especially since it is by no means mandatory by anyone. We now live in an age where we can protect the tribe from outsiders without taking those forms. Your brother and sister triggered their curses by accident. They had no intention of doing it. But now here you stand wanting to trigger it. Why?"

It was funny that he mentioned Daba and Phala triggering their curses like it really was the burden it was when the curse was placed on those lucky few. Yet both of them were looked at like things out of legend, adored beyond comprehension. "Father, with all due respect I don't think anyone who has the meqa-moya gene in them and has triggered it can understand why I need to do this."

Judging by the disappointed look on his face, Impi didn't like this answer. Although it appeared to be more because he still didn't understand rather than because he didn't want him to go.

"Inkosi," said the councilman known as Bab' Sizwa. "With respect, I think if the boy wants to go then he should be allowed to go. As long as he understands the dangers out there then there's no reason to—"

He was cut off by another councilman name Bab' Qino. "The boy doesn't understand," he said authoritatively. "He's being foolish and thoughtless. These actions are unbecoming of a son of the King."

"Careful," said another councilman named Bab' Maphakathi. "That's the King's son you're speaking about, Qino. And if he hasn't prepared himself for what lies ahead, he shall need to deal with that himself." Bab' Maphakathi turned to address Sando. "The only way to become a man of this tribe is to face your problems."

"Indeed," said Bab' Sizwa. "Which is why I feel the boy must go."

Qino made a disapproving sound. "This may as well be a death-sentence."

"These were traditions once upon a time," said another councilman and another one answered. The council continued to argue while Impi considered his options in his mind before silencing the council.

"Thulani madoda." Impi always commanded respect when he spoke in that voice. He looked directly at Sando. "I have decided. I will grant you permission to go on a spirit walk. You will leave here a boy and journey where your spirit guides you and return a man. But a word of caution. You cannot go to the Nite Pole. You know as well as every man and woman in the Bantulands what lies there, and I will not have a member of my tribe commit the same mistakes the foreigners did three hundred years ago."

"I understand father."

Impi continued. "Ignite the curse if you can, but if you can't, do not think less of yourself as when you return you will be a man, my son. When the sun goes down, your brother will take you to Mlumbi who will prepare you for the journey. Until then rest easy my son." Sando was about to leave when Impi added one last thing. "But before you go just remember this:

By Bernard Bayede

when you're out there you stand alone. None of us can help you so listen to your spirit, trust your instincts and remember everything you were taught about surviving."

"Yes Inkosi," he said before adding, "and thank you father."

*

Sando had hardly been able to contain his excitement from the moment he got out of the council hut. But he hadn't wasted time. He'd hurried to his sleeping hut to pack a bag before hurrying down to the blacksmiths at the armory to mend his weapons to perfection. He realized how overzealous he was as he was all done before midday and was now stuck with nothing to do for the rest of the day.

Fortunately, enough, Phala had found him and convinced him to test his new spear out in a duel before he headed out. Sando considered the fact that this could very well be the last time he ever saw his older sister and relented. An hour later, they were standing across from each other in the snow field where the tribe warriors trained, with their double-bladed spears trained in front of them in their stances.

They had now changed into sparring armor which consisted of dried animal hide that had been hardened through boiling. It was much lighter than their normal clothes and thus also much more susceptible to the weather. Of course, the idea was that the wearer wouldn't be still enough to feel the cold. It covered their torso and thighs leaving their arms and lower legs exposed.

Phala wore a smile on her face. "So," she said as she began the footwork that saw them circling each other, "did you know that in Emperia, they call these blade staffs."

"Oh please. Those foreigners only know of their swords." Sando moved his spear blocking and parrying his sister's moves. Phala smiled recognizing the white crystal-coated weapon which now matched hers. "I see you've upgraded your weapon."

"I got special permission. You know, with this possibly being the last of me and all that."

"Careful now. If you start doubting yourself, then you stop thinking about your opponent's moves and only think of your own!" Phala proved her point with a quick succession of moves that ended with the edge of her blade nicking Sando's shoulder. Phala smiled. "And you're right by the way. Emperians tried our so-called blade staffs and found that they had no patience to learn the fine art of how to use it." Phala had flipped through the air, landing on the other side of Sando. However, when she landed, Sando twirled his spear at just the right time and angle that he nicked Phala's arm.

"What is this? Have the mighty fallen?"

"Don't get cocky, brother." They exchanged more moves, showing themselves to be evenly matched. "So, have you given any thoughts to where you're going to go?"

"I don't decide, you know that. I have to follow my spirit. But I do know where I can't go."

"The Nite Pole." They'd spoke then words in unison as they continued to spar. The story of the Nite Pole and what lay there was legendary among all the Bantu people and it dated all the way back the Great Voyage of 492. The foreigners of Emperia had arrived by ship on the shores of the Bantulands and claimed that they were here in search of gold crystals buried deep under their lands. Since the Bantu people cared not for the shiny rocks as they had no power, they allowed them to mine the precious rocks.

Weeks turned to months which turned to years and the tribes learnt from the foreigners. Unfortunately, the arrangement quickly proved to be not without its flaws when the foreigners began exploring the land and taking excursions further and further nite until they reached the Nite Pole. And as the story goes, they found evil there because following these excursions to the Nite Pole, conflict arose between them and Bantu people that left a permanent resentment between the

113

tribesmen and any outsiders. Now, only the Kwanza dared to even tolerate their presence.

The fight finally came to an end when Sando managed to cut Phala across her midsection, causing blood to drip onto the snow: the universal sign of victory for the one who caused the cut. The strength of Sando's now-indestructible blade had caused Phala's torso armor to be cut clean in half leaving her midriff bare.

When Sando turned around to the sight of a few of the younger tribesman who had gathered to watch the duel enjoying the sight of his sister's toned tummy, he grimaced. "Sorry sister."

"No worries, brother." She touched the wound and looked up at the sky. "I'll heal when the moon comes up." She then gestured at their spectators. "And then we'll see if these boys are still amused with me then." She watched their faces change to ones of worry. "That's what I thought." She planted her spear in the ground expertly and came up to Sando for a more private word. "I see you've improved. That's the first time you've beat me in a fight."

Sando gave her an amused look. "I don't think that true, sister."

"I mean without cheating." Phala was recalling their earlier fights where Sando had won by throwing snow in her eyes or pretending to surrender. Not counting those instances, this would be the first time that Sando had won a duel against her. "I dare say that I think that you're ready, brother."

Sando smiled. "Just in time."

After changing back into more appropriate clothing, Phala escorted Sando back into the village where most of the tribe had gathered to give Sando a final send-off. The send-off was no small thing as an entire event was made out of it with performances put on that would only be seen at weddings or the birth of a prince.

First there were the dancers, all youthful women, dressed in beautiful yet revealing outfits that were made completely out of seashells of various shades of blue. The dancers showed their youth with their long and rhythmic performance, the shells rattling with their moves to create energetic rattling beats.

Not to be outdone, their performance was immediately followed by male dancers, dressed in various sea animal hides, who showed off more powerful moves with hard foot work to complement their baritone chants. This was accompanied by loud drumming performed on drums made out of wood and hide. When the ceremony was over, King Impi gave a farewell speech before introducing his other son as the man who would escort Sando out of the village to the sound of cheers.

Daba Golide, like Sando and Impi before him, had a powerful build. And with a dark brown complexion, long dreadlocks and a full beard, Daba was the spitting image of a young Impi. However, when Daba smiled, there were no wrinkles to speak of. Daba greeted his brother and told Sando to come with him.

"So," said Sando as they walked, "why did father ask you to take me to Mlumbi. I mean, I know where his hut is."

"Yes, but when a tribesman is about to go on a spirit walk, it's custom for the King to walk the tribesman to see the tribe wielder."

"Again, same question."

"Well since this is one of those once in a lifetime events, father thought it would be more important for me to take you to the wielder."

"Well as the next King, that makes sense."

"Aha." Daba gave him a big smile like he used to when they were kids. "Let me ask you something, when are you going to get a woman?"

Sando usually rolled his eyes when Daba asked this question but he was curious this time. "What's the point of asking me that now?"

"Because I have faith that you're coming back. And when you do, I want to know that you're going to find love."

"Here we go. You know something brother, we can't all have a Nanda in our lives." Nanda and Daba had been friends since they were children. When they grew up, that naturally turned into love and now she was destined to be their next queen.

Daba laughed. "You always say that."

Sando also laughed. "Well, it's true."

"Listen little brother. Becoming meqa-moya is all well and good but being a warrior means nothing if you haven't got something to protect."

"But there is something to protect: the tribe. You know what father always says. 'Tribesmen live and die but the tribe lives on forever'. So, isn't this woman you want me to find also just a tribesman who will eventually die? Protecting the tribe is surely more important."

This time it was Daba who rolled his eyes. "Good Light, listen to yourself. Sando, you've..." But he trailed off.

"I've got to what?"

"Nothing. I just realized: you're going on a spirit walk. Which means I don't need to convince you of anything. When you come back, you'll have all your answers."

"Here's to hoping."

They kept going until they were behind the hill that formed the edge of the village and right there, at the end of a path that went through a small forest of trees, was a hut standing in isolation. This hut belonged to the sole Pula tribesman in the Golide village. Following the treaty, the Golide, Kwanza and Kwacha tribes each had at least one Pula tribesman that they allowed to stay with them who was also a wielder. Since the Pula were the only wielders in the Bantulands and all the tribes were in agreement that it was a good idea to have a wielder among them, this had become the norm.

When they reached the hut, Daba knocked on the door only to find a hooded figure standing behind them." As I live and breathe, amadodana amakhosi."

"Mlumbi," said Daba in a serious tone. It was only after the wielder took off his hood to reveal an old man with snow white hair and matching beard that Daba broke into a smile, having feigned his serious tone. He embraced the man. "How you are doing, old man?"

"Old, huh?" he said breaking into a jolly laugh. "Is it that I am too old or that you two are so young."

Sando rolled his eyes. "You and your philosophies," he said giving the wielder a smile and hug of his own.

"Oh, it's just a wise old saying."

Sando and Daba shared a knowing look, having so many throughout their childhood. "How many wise old sayings do you have?"

"Well, a wise old man once told me never to reveal all my secrets."

"Was he older than you?" joked Daba. Mlumbi laughed.

"What else did that old man tell you?" asked Sando.

"That one day, a son of a King would come to me and on that day, I would prepare him for a journey like no other."

Sando gave him a look before laughing. "No one told you that. Come on now."

"Actually, they did," confirmed Mlumbi. "Prophecies are a common skill with experienced wielders. And my predecessor told me, long ago, that one day, I would have the extraordinary honor of bestowing a special young man with the knowledge and guidance he needs to go through a spirit walk."

Sando looked to his older brother to see if knew of this only to see that this was the first Daba was hearing this. Sando turned back to Mlumbi. "So that means you knew all this time that this would eventually happen; that I would be here, today, talking to you?"

Mlumbi let out another one of his jolly old-man laughs. "Oh no. Remember, it wasn't my prophecy. Which means, like you, I had to wait and see how things would play out. But truth be told, as the day of the prophecy grew closer and closer and I became wiser and wiser, I came to understand where my path was leading."

It dawned on Sando that he'd gravely underestimated Mlumbi as just another Pula tribesman who had all this power of which he didn't know what to do with. As it turned out, he was worthy of his power. "And what about my path? Do you know where this spirit walk is going to take me?"

Mlumbi smiled and held out an arm. "Come. It's time for your journey to begin." Leaving Daba to wait at the hut, Mlumbi led Sando back through the small forest before they came to a formation of rocks. On the other side was a pond of water Sando was surprised to have known nothing about. "As I'm sure you already know, the journey you are about to take is not about direction so where you go cannot be dictated by you nor anyone else. Only your spirit can guide you."

Sando was aware of this concept but he still needed more than that. "And how will I know when my spirit is guiding me? Will I hear a voice in my head; will I see a shooting star in the sky…?"

Mlumbi muffled his jolly laugh this time. "Oh, it will be more subtle than that but with a little help from a rune, it will also be clearer."

"A rune? What's that?"

Mlumbi immediately answered his question by producing a small yellow crystal which he held in the palm of his open hand. "As I've already taught you as a boy, a yellow crystal, when split in two, allows two wielders to communicate over long distances. How this works is that the crystal opens up a wielder's mind to other wielders but connects them to the other wielder with the crystal's twin. Through centuries of study, we have found that when the yellow crystal is crushed into a fine powder and consumed by a person with power in their blood, such as a prince with a meqa-moya gene, it opens their minds too."

This was news to Sando. Mlumbi had left that out of the teachings he gave him and his siblings as a boy. "Wait, are you saying that we can communicate across long distances too?"

Mlumbi let out another muffled laugh, shaking his head. "The yellow powder can only open the mind. Connecting it is another story. That's where this comes in." Mlumbi opened his other palm to reveal a small black crystal no bigger than the yellow crystal. "A black crystal is one of the trickiest crystals to master for a wielder because it requires a wielder to resist the Darkness in order to use it properly. Its power allows a wielder to put a mind, a body or a soul to sleep. Through study, a wielder can learn many ways of using it, all of which are dangerous."

Sando remembered these lessons and remembered finding them fascinating as the applications had seemed endless. While standard uses could see a wielder simply put an enemy – or even a friend – to sleep by touching them with it, Sando had realized a more ingenious wielder who also had a red crystal that allowed them to move things with their mind, could put a person to sleep without touching them.

Mlumbi continued. "Centuries ago, the wielders of the Pula tribe discovered that when a black crystal is turned into a paste and painted on an individual with power in their blood, it binds their minds with their ancestors."

Sando was lost. "What? I don't understand."

"The power in the crystal is a manifestation of slumber in all its various forms. Now our beliefs as Bantu is that our ancestors aren't truly dead but rather in an eternal sleep with their spirits living on in the Heavens. The power of the crystal allows you as a royal tribe member with power in their blood, to connect with them. Do you understand?"

Sando wasn't sure that he did, but he was too eager to hear the punchline. "Uh, my mind can connect to their dreams?"

This time Mlumbi didn't muffle his jolly laugh. "Good Light, I've never heard it put so simply but yes, that's basically it. Now," he said kneeling down and picking up a small bowl that had been sitting by the side of the pond all this time, "when you combine these two phenomena, you will find that you will be able to communicate directly with your ancestor and thus, be able to hear your spirit guide you."

Sando was still trying to get his head around the science of what he'd just been told as Mlumbi quickly crushed the yellow crustal into a powder in the bowl before adding water from the pond and giving it to Sando to drink. As Sando forced the bitter drink down, he thought more about it and realized that this wasn't about science at all. This was about something beyond science so perhaps he should simply trust that the process would work.

Once Sando was done with the bowl, Mlumbi took it back and immediately crushed the black crystal into it. The black crystal proved to be a lot tougher to work with as it was stickier. So, when Mlumbi mixed in the pond water, it turned into a sticky paste rather than a drinkable solution. Mlumbi asked Sando to expose his left arm and then dipped two fingers into it and painted a figure that looked like a bowing bird onto his arm.

A moment passed with nothing happening. "Is it not working?"

"It takes some time."

"So, then what do we do, wait?"

Another jolly laugh. "*I* am going to my hut to eat some fish that just arrived from Pula. Mmm, my favorite," he mused. "*You* have a long journey ahead of you, so you better get going."

Sando was lost. "Go where? I thought my ancestor was going to start speaking to me and tell me where to go."

"Well, you have to put in *some* effort too. Remember, this spirit walk is designed to turn you into a man. To be a man, you're going to have to have an instinct on what to do. That starts now."

To Sando's surprise, those were Mlumbi's parting words as he started back for his hut. Sando followed a minute later and was glad to find that Daba was still there. He asked what happened.

"Well apparently, I have to start this walk on my own whim after all."

"Well, I'm not worried. After almost eighteen years of living on these lands, I'm sure you have enough instincts to know the best routes to take."

Thinking about it, Sando realized that he did have an idea of which way he'd go. He looked far into the distance, up at the mountains to the nite and pointed. "Well, I've always wanted to see what's up there."

Daba hesitated before smiling, seemingly deciding to trust his brother. "Well as long as you don't get curious as to what's on the other side." Daba outstretched his arms. "Brother, I wish you well and may you come back a man."

Sando smiled at his older brother and embraced him. "Thank you Daba. And farewell."

With all the goodbyes now done, Sando picked up his bag of supplies, slung them onto his back and started away from the only home he knew. He could still feel the cold of where Mlumbi had marked him, but it was gradually getting warmer. Sando thought of the journey ahead and wondered how long it was going to take him: a week? Regardless, he'd set him mind on it: he was going to the top of the Nite Mountains – the same mountains that stood between the tribes and the Nite Pole!

*

As Sando navigated the narrow path alongside the steep hillside, he thought about what it must have been like where spirit walks were a regular occurrence and a mandatory of rite passage. Did each and every boy of the tribe have to choose their own path to begin? It was no wonder that there was a startlingly high death count for spirit walks. Allegedly, almost everyone was happy when the tribe did away with the spirit walk a hundred years ago. But now, here Sando was, bringing the dangerous concept back to life.

It had been a few days since Sando had left the village and while progress was slow, today, it was finally looking like he was making progress as the mountain was much closer. Every night, he'd been forced to put up a tent for shelter but as he got closer and closer to the mountains, there was more and more wind. Sando was afraid that he was closing in on a snowstorm in which case a tent would do him no good and he'd have to put up a snow hut.

Fortunately, as he navigated the snowy hillside, he came across an opening in the rocks. When he went inside, he was pleasantly surprised to find that it was a cave which would provide him shelter for the night.

By the looks of the cave, it belonged to a wild animal which, judging from the skeleton, was long dead. Sando pulled the dead bird he'd killed earlier in the day off his back and prepared to cook it.

As he settled down with his food, Sando thought about the legendary spirit walks he'd heard about when he was younger. While they'd been many, the most memorable were those of the royal family, his family. In fact, before the spirit walk was done away with completely, it was the Golide tribe that continued the tradition as it began: to transition into something done to trigger the curse. Those were the last spirit walkers of the Bantu people.

Of all those stories, there was none more legendary than that of the Kings Three. And like all legendary stories, it was a tragic tale. Taking place two hundred years ago and a century after the Great Voyage, it was a story of how the sons of three kings decided to go on a spirit walk together and to mark how special the moment was, they decided to do something unprecedented: travel across the sea.

Chemba – the son of the King of the Kwacha; Konga – the son of the King of the Kwanza; and Yetu – the son of the King of the Golide had convinced their fathers to allow them to go together as all three wanted to become meqa-moya and believed that their spirits were calling them across the sea. So, the three boarded a small ship and set off, eventually making land on what seemed like an uninhabited jungle land. They would learn quickly that this place was Tandem Solaris. And it was not uninhabited.

Even centuries ago, the Bantu people were aware that the Solari were dangerous people but not for being fearsome warriors but rather for their keen ability to train dangerous and mysterious beasts known as tandemites. Tandemites were known for three things: being evolved from the daminites that fell from the sky over eight hundred years ago; being vicious killing machines; and being completely obedient to the Solari. So, when Chemba, Konga and Yetu came across one such beast, they knew that they were in trouble.

Described as big black furless dogs with red eyes and sharp claws that stood taller than an average man, the Kings Three were certain that their deaths were imminent until the unthinkable happened and Chemba triggered his curse and became a meqa-moya just in time to defend his friends. But the tandemite proved too strong and Chemba was killed which eventually proved to be the moment that the War of the Claws began.

As Sando tried to get some sleep, he compared his situation with that of the Kings Three. His situation wasn't so bad in retrospect. At least he wasn't leaving the country. And he knew these lands. He knew the kind of threats he would run into and there were no tandemites here. Of course, it was the presence of the tandemite and the need to fight it that allowed Chemba to become a meqa-moya in the first place. So, did that mean he was also destined to have to fight in order to fulfil his own destiny? The idea gave Sando something to think about as he drifted off to sleep.

When he woke up the next morning, he went about his morning routine of unpacking the maizemeal he'd packed and making porridge for breakfast, preparing himself for the day. He found himself becoming agitated by the mark on his arm. He wondered if Mlumbi had put it on properly before ignoring it and getting on with his day.

The day went on without a problem as it appeared that the coming storm had passed him by but only barely. It appeared that the area between him and the mountains was generally storm-ridden so Sando tried to pick up the pace. Fortunately, the area was becoming more and more rocky which made finding caves easier. And while he couldn't always find a cave, when he didn't, he'd manage to find suitable area to make a makeshift snow hut with the help of his tenting tools.

As the days had gone past, Sando had felt his mark burning more and more. It finally came to a point where he felt that it was going to explode, and he took off his furs to find that the mark was glowing like lava as if it was on fire. It was the middle of the night, so Sando couldn't see if the mark was now burnt into his skin. However, not a moment later, the few clouds that were in the night sky, parted to reveal the moon and the mark immediately stopped burning. Instead, something else started happening.

The powerful red-orange glow had lifted like a ball of light, right off Sando's skin and moved in front of him like it was a large dragonfly glowing in the night. The light travelled ahead of him a few meters and Sando followed it like a lite-star before it suddenly went straight down into the ground... except that it wasn't the ground at all. Instead of snow, Sando saw that he was now standing on a frozen lake.

With the lake looking like it had been frozen for years, Sando was far less concerned with any mortal danger and more concerned with the light which he realized he could still see glowing beneath the surface. That's impossible. Sando kneeled to get a closer look and swore that he could see a person beneath the ice. He swept away the layer of snow on the ice until he could see his own reflection when his eyes suddenly popped open. In the reflection, there was someone standing right over him.

Sando looked up and jumped back, falling to the ground. "Who in lloomis are you!?"

The man smiled. "I'm the one you've been waiting for. I'm the one who will guide you the rest of the way." Judging by the man's powerful build along with his long dreadlocks, black beard and striking resemblance to Impi, Daba and himself, Sando deduced that he was a royal member of the Golide tribe: an ancestor. His similar fur clothing was also a dead giveaway that he was from the Golide tribe.

"You're my spirit?" said Sando in awe.

The man, still smiling, shook his head. "I'm your spirit guide. Your spirit lives in you. I am just how you interpret what it's telling you."

"And what is it telling me?"

The man didn't answer immediately. "What you seek is not out there, on that mountain. It's inside you, Sando."

Sando pondered that. "You mean the gene inside me. Yes, I know. I am out here because I want to activate it. I want to trigger the curse."

The man shook his head again. "I speak of your strength, Sando. That's what you truly seek: the strength to be a worthy enough man for your tribe."

"Yes, and I believe that the way to do that is to become meqa-moya. Can you guide me to becoming one?"

The man did not lose his smile, but he did take a long, deep breath as if those were not the words that he'd wanted to hear come out of Sando's mouth. Regardless, he continued in being a spirit guide. "To obtain the power that you seek, consider the heart and remember that whatever does not break from the cracks can only help to make it stronger. And that strength is the one you seek to be worthy."

Sando didn't understand. "What?" Unfortunately, the man momentarily disappeared like a shadow in the light. "Wait, I don't understand."

He blinked away again before coming back. "You will when the time comes." His blinking became more frequent.

Sando was becoming desperate. "Wait, wait, wait. You never told me who you are!?"

The man's smile widened as if he knew he was about to leave forever. "Yetu. My name is Yetu." Yetu then finally disappeared, leaving an awe-struck Sando sitting with a shocked expression on his face. Yetu was one of the most legendary members of the Golide royal family and one of the Kings Three.

Before Sando could truly contemplate the idea that his spirit guide was none other than Yetu Golide, he found himself suddenly in a tactical mindset. Standing right there, not thirty meters in front of him was a polar bear and it looked hungry. Sando hadn't seen it before because Yetu's image had been blocking it from view.

With it being a full moon, Sando could see it perfectly and now it could see him. While Sando's instinct was to flee, as he'd been taught in his hunting lessons as a young boy (polar bears were not to be messed with when they were hungry or angry) another more ambitious thought crossed his mind. What if this is it!?

While Sando could not begin to understand what his spirit guide had been talking about with breaks and cracks, he did understand the history of his people. He remembered the story of how Chemba had triggered his curse and how it had been the threat of the tandemite that had done it for him. Perhaps this was his test! Perhaps this bear and the threat it posed to his life would trigger his curse. While there was no way of knowing for sure, Sando was willing to take the gamble.

He'd been carrying his spear in his hand the whole trip as it didn't fit in his pack so now it was easy access. Sando dropped his bag and started forward with his spear, walking gingerly. As soon as he was close enough, the bear swung its arm at him which Sando ducked. Making use of his footwork, Sando parried the bears attacks before managing to cut it just underneath the arm. This angered the bear!

It let out a deafening growl and Sando knew that he had to put space between it and him. He began running away and it chased him. It closed the gap fast but when it lunged, Sando attempted to somersault backwards over it. Unfortunately, due to the bear's sheer size, the move wasn't clean, and he ended up tumbling over its back. However, Sando recovered by swinging his spear as hard as he could managing to make a deep cut across its face.

The cut had gone through its left eye and nose. The pain must have been excruciating as it let out an even louder growl, now even angrier. But this time, Sando didn't run. Instead, he moved to the bear's left, attempting to keep to the bear's new blind spot. This proved affective as Sando began landing some good cuts. But the bear's flesh was too thick for the quick strokes he was making. He needed more powerful strikes which required getting much closer.

Noticing the bear was becoming more and more irritated, Sando ignored this and started moving around it, trying to stay close. As he tried to measure it for a good cut, he thought about his goal. He wondered what he had to do to trigger his curse. As he continued to ponder this, the bear let out its frustration by smashing its front legs so hard that there was an audible crack followed by smaller crackles... it was the ice. The bear had cracked the ice.

Now forced to move far more carefully, the bear seemed to notice this and turned its action into a tactic and banged its front legs on the ice over and over again. Sando wondered if he shouldn't just let the bear break the ice and end itself but then realized that surely that wouldn't make him meqa-moya and instead, decided to make his move.

Keeping his steps light, Sando charged at the bear while it was still banging its legs. He aimed for its heart, wondering if perhaps, that's what Yetu meant with his last words. However, just before he could land his blow, the bear turned around and swung its claw at him and finally managed to hurt him!

The bear had driven its right claw into Sando's belly causing him to drop the spear. It was over. It was all over… at least Sando thought it was but it appeared the bear didn't believe so. It lifted Sando's body up and began swinging him around violently as if now trying to get him off its claw. It eventually started banging him on the ice before Sando eventually detached from its claw.

As Sando lay there not moving due to the immense pain he was feeling, he couldn't help but wonder just how badly he'd failed. This was his trial and he failed. He'd failed to become meqa-moya and he'd failed his tribe. Unfortunately, it seemed that the bear wasn't done as it looked at him as if noticing that he wasn't dead and prepared for the kill. As the bear let out another deafening growl, Sando took note of something peculiar. The ice where he'd been thrown had broken, allowing him to feel the water under the surface and that water was warm.

Desperate to survive, Sando did the only thing he could and banged his own fist on the ice, but it didn't break. He tried again, still nothing. He wasn't strong enough. That's when he got an idea and waited until the bear went for its fatal stomp. At the last possible moment, Sando rolled out of the way, letting the bear stomp right through the ice making a hole in the ice. When the bear stood back up, Sando rolled back to where he'd been just moments before and allowed himself to fall through the hole.

Now underwater, Sando began to wave his hands and legs about, holding his breath and looking back up through the hole. He watched as the frustrated bear wondered what happened to him. Either not eager to swim or believing Sando had truly disappeared, the bear let out one last frustrated growl and left running. When Sando was sure that it was far enough away he surfaced.

By Bernard Bayede

He crawled out of the hole and fought the pain coming from his wounds. For a moment he lay on the ice, just thanking *The Light* he was alive. He wondered why the lake was warm and thought back to any lessons Mlumbi might have given on the subject. The only thing he could think of was that one time when the wielder had said that while the Bantulands were known for their abundance of gold crystals that there were in fact other kinds of crystals there, but they were located too close to the Nite Pole.

Was it then possible, considering how close he was to the Nite Pole right now, that there were perhaps blue sparking crystals deep under the lake that were keeping the water warm? Even as he thought about it, Sando recognized that it was a crazy idea. But how else to explain the phenomenon?

Sando heard another growl close by and looked up to find that the bear was still on the frozen lake albeit far across the ice. But it was on the lite side of the lake meaning that it was between Sando and his way home. Not wanting to mess with the bear again, Sando crawled to the nite side of the lake and was thankful to find rocks forming the boarder on the other side. He was even more thankful to find that those rocks were warm, seemingly being affected by the same source of heat as the lake.

As Sando lay there, he realized that his injuries were fatal and that if he didn't get help, he was going to die. Unfortunately, he was also losing consciousness. Realizing his doomed predicament, Sando simply lay there, looking at the moon. He wondered what he'd done wrong. He thought about Yetu as the edge of unconsciousness closed in on him. This was it. This was the end.

*

Sando had always struggled to find meaning in dreams even after Mlumbi had told him how important they were and how they had meaning. Sando wondered what the meaning of this one was as he stood in the middle of a jungle. Looking around, he noticed that there seemed to be a clearing up ahead.

Curious, Sando approached it. But before he stepped out of the trees, he heard a commotion.

"My Lady, step back. I don't want to hurt you."

"My love, I won't let you go through this alone."

"No. Don't come any closer. It's happening."

"Oh, my love."

Having heard enough and eager to know what was happening, Sando stepped into the clearing just in time to see Yetu, doubled over in front of a beautiful woman with long black hair and coal-black eyes. Judging from her light brown complexion and dress made from the hide of animals not found in the Bantulands, she was Solari. That's when Sando remembered how the War of the Claws truly broke out… when Yetu accidently killed the daughter of a Solari chief.

True to the legendary story, Yetu transformed in front of Sando's very eyes into a giant wolf-like beast, except it looked like no wolf. Its fur was disheveled and white; it's eyes a light illuminous blue and its canine teeth, so sharp and so long that it was impossible for its mouth to close properly. It was also so big that it was taller than a man, standing on all fours. This was a meqa-moya.

To Sando's horror, the Solari Lady was still standing awfully close to the meqa-moya and seemed to be unafraid as she held her hands out and concentrated. It appeared that she was trying to pet it. But whatever she was doing was not working as the meqa-moya looked to be getting agitated and all of a sudden looked up and howled. That was when Sando noticed the moon which looked breath-takingly large in the clear night sky and seemed to shine brighter than the rings which were also glowing in the distance.

Sando was brought back to the scene in front of him when the meqa-moya suddenly spun around to run off but did so fast that the Solari Lady went flying through the air and bounced off a tree with an audible crack. The force of the impact had snapped her neck. Yetu had killed her. But judging from what happened, it was clear that it was an accident.

By Bernard Bayede

The dream suddenly fizzled to broad daylight and Sando saw Yetu return to the clearing to find his dead wife and cradled her body. Sando saw how devastated he was and couldn't help but feel sorry for him. He had killed the love of his life by complete accident and effectively started a war.

Sando remembered the stories of this dark time in the history of his people and he remembered that it was always glossed over. It was clear that even the Bantu people were not proud of this series of events as very few of them knew the whole story. But surely, he wasn't the first one to have this vision of the past? Of course, mistake or not, the death of a chief's daughter was never going to go unpunished. Sando now remembered her name: Lady Lakewalker. He also remembered why it was so significant.

While the current state of the Solari people had them divided into five tribes not dissimilar to the Bantu people, that had once been one tribe. An entire nation ruled by one leader who was known only as Lakewalker. Sando vaguely remembered his call to fame being that he once traversed the surface of a lake to defeat some sort of beast. But since this story wasn't about his people, Sando had never cared to remember the finer details. What he did remember was that, following the marriage of his descendant to Yetu; her death at his hands and the war that followed, the Solari people became as divided as the Bantu people and nothing has been the same since.

However, that was three hundred years ago and didn't help Sando's situation now. It was the legend of Lakewalker and his battle on a lake that reminded Sando of his own failed battle and the fact that he was currently dying. Having had enough of the dream world, Sando opened his eyes, barely managing the effort and saw that the sun was out and he was also moving but not under his own power. He tried to see who was moving him but when he blinked, it was dark again and he was no longer moving.

Sando tried to sit up but found that he couldn't so instead he rolled over and saw what looked like someone building a snow hut. By the looks of it, it was a woman, but he couldn't be sure because everything was blurry. When he blinked to consciousness again, it was light again, and they were inside the snow hut. He tried to speak but the blurry woman hushed him and told him to get some sleep.

The next time Sando woke up, things were clearer, and he noticed that he was in a cave. They must have moved again which made Sando wonder just how much time passed since the bear had defeated him. He tried to sit up again only to find that he couldn't. It was his wound. It hurt when he moved which he found interesting. He realized that it must have been better now because it didn't hurt when he was dead still. But moving also gave him a splitting headache.

The woman came into the cave and saw him moving. "No, don't move," she said. "I've sown your wounds closed and if you move, you will tear them open again."

Sando vaguely recognized her accent but not as being from here but rather from his dream. Looking at the slightly less blurry image of the woman, he saw that she had the same long black hair and light brown complexion of the Solari. "Lady Lakewalker?" But Sando feinted before he could get an answer.

The next time Sando woke up, he was feeling much better. While his wounds still hurt when he tried to get up, he no longer had the splitting headache, and everything was clear. When the woman came into the cave, Sando wondered if he was still hallucinating. Was Lady Lakewalker really here? However, when she took off the hooded cloak that was covering her head, Sando realized that this was a complete stranger to him… a Solari stranger.

Sando closed the gap between them and the woman dropped the firewood she'd been carrying when he started choking her. "Who are you!?" he said in Emperian. He remembered his father insisted that all his family members – and any other tribe member that wanted to – learn the language of the foreigners, wanting to make sure that his people weren't left behind by the rest of the world.

"Don't kill me," said the woman, also in Emperian. "Please, I'm not here to hurt you."

"Then why are you here? What are you doing on Bantu land?"

The woman struggled to speak with Sando's grip on her. "I'm trying to save your life." Unfortunately, she was not believed and Sando squeezed leaving the Solari woman to do the only thing she could to get him to let go and punched him in the gut, right where his wound was. Sando immediately doubled over. "I'm not trying to hurt you," she coughed out. "I'm trying to save your life."

"By punching me?"

"You were choking me, remember?"

"Yes, because you're in the wrong country," he said, accepting that his strength hadn't returned and sitting back down.

"Well perhaps you can punish me after you get better, yes?"

Sando couldn't help but be amused by her sarcasm. It was the last thing he expected from people he'd been told never to trust. In fact, it was the kind of humor that his tribe would expect from him. He quickly accepted that she wasn't a threat. "Are you alone?" he asked, trying to assess the situation.

"That depends on your meaning. If you count the reindeer just outside—"

"Reindeer?" asked Sando. He remembered that that was what the Emperian foreigners called cold weather antelope. "Is that how you got here?" When she nodded, Sando laughed only to instantly regret it when his wounds began to pull. "You're the first person I've met to ride a reindeer."

The woman gave him a face that Sando had to admit was surprising attractive. "I'll have you know that I was actually riding a sled." This time it was Sando that made a face, surprised. "How do you think I was able to travel with you?"

"It takes at least four to get anywhere out here."

153

The woman realized that he had assumed she only had one. "Reindeer can mean one or many, yes?"

Sando rolled his eyes. "Yes, I know that. I just didn't think you could gather four reindeer; build yourself a sled and get all the way out here by yourself."

"Well, you thought wrong."

Another question occurred to Sando. "Where are we?"

"We're halfway up the mountain."

Sando thought about that. "We're nite of the lake?" She nodded. "Why did you take us this way? How close are we to the Nite Pole?"

"Well, there was a very big bear on the other side of the lake. And we're nowhere near the Nite Pole, assuming it's on the other side of the mountain." She saw the look on his face. "It's a very big mountain and I wasn't going to drag you all the way over it."

"Then why did you even drag me halfway up it?"

"They're more caves the higher we go. And since they're more snowstorms out here, I preferred to be in a cave than in a snow hut. Don't you agree?"

Sando could tell that she wasn't really happy with him and she rubbed her throat as if to indicate that she hadn't forgiven him for attacking her. Unfortunately for her, forgiveness was not something Golide were known for seeking so Sando changed the subject. "You still haven't told me what you're doing out here in the Bantulands."

"I'm looking for absolution. Judging from the look on your face, it would appear you are too." Sando didn't answer and she took that as the truth. "My name is Katalie Kayne by the way," she said smiling.

*

After introducing himself, Sando and Katalie got to talking and Katalie revealed that it was now the 1st of Uranus meaning that it had been almost a month since he left home and three weeks since he'd been injured. They spent the rest of the day talking about the journey up the mountain with Sando commending Katalie on her bravery but also pointing out the basic survival mistakes she'd made.

As the days passed, they'd managed to keep their conversations about their survival and his recovery but every day, Sando would ask what she was doing there. After a week, Sando had become strong enough to go with her to gather firewood and hunt for food. Sando had noticed that every day, she'd come back with a dead bird which they'd eat for supper and now he finally knew how she did it: supernaturally.

"No, I'm not a wielder," she said over the fire as they cooked the bird.

"Really? Because you brought that bird right to us with only your mind and it barely fought when you snapped it's neck. What is that if not wielder power?"

"It's a gift that all Solari have, at least those that are taught how to do it properly."

"And what skill is that?"

Katalie smiled which, unbeknown to her, brightened Sando's day. "The Bantu people aren't the only ones who believe in a spirit world, you know."

"I take it you're not talking about the other dimensions hidden in the rings."

She shook her head. "No, I'm talking about the ability to have your spirit communicate with someone else's spirit. That's how it seems that I can control the actions of the birds. I can't control them, but my spirit can talk with theirs. That's how I managed to round up the reindeer."

It just occurred to Sando that that was what Lady Lakewalker was trying to do with Yetu when he was in his meqa-moya form. She'd been trying to communicate with him, believing that his spirit was still in the beast. But another thought popped into Sando's mind. "Is that why those tandemite creatures are so obedient to you? Your spirits communicate with theirs?"

157

Katalie's facial expression notably changed. "No, communicating with the spirits of those beasts is a talent left to cursors."

"Ker-saws?"

"Cursors are Solari that dedicate their entire lives to training tandemites. But the rest of us believe it to be a dangerous thing to do because tandemites come from daminites and many people believe that the daminites are not of *The Light* so we stay away. And fortunately, so do cursors as they tend to stay in the jungle."

Sando found himself deeply intrigues by this story. "So, is that why you came here? You ran away from Tandem Solaris because of these cursors?"

Katalie shook her head, her expression changing again. She sighed, finally giving in to this ongoing interrogation. "I came here because I had to get away. I had to get away from the politics of our tribe and the inevitable path that I was destined to end up on." When Sando gave her a confused look, she continued.

"Sando, I'm royalty. I'm the daughter of Kaizer Kayne, the chief of the Ignis Tribe."

This time it was Sando's face that changed. And it had changed because everything had changed. If Katalie was royalty, that means she had abandoned her people, leaving them without a future leader. The disappointment in Sando could not be described. For his entire life, the one thing that had been drilled into Sando was tribe loyalty and now here he was listening to this beautiful woman confessing to being a disloyal deserter.

Unfortunately, Sando's disappointment manifested itself as anger. "So, what you're saying is that you abandoned your people rather than take up your responsibility?"

"Sando, it's not that simple."

"It sounds simple to me. You deserted your people."

"No, I didn't."

"Katalie, you were the daughter of the chief and instead of taking your place as their ruler, you ran away."

"I wasn't his heir," spat Katalie. Seeing that this calmed Sando down, she continued on. "No, that would be my step-brother."

"Oh."

However, Katalie continued, lest he didn't understand the full picture. "And he was a cruel man. But you see, he wasn't always my stepbrother. Once upon a time, he was my lover." Seeing the horrified look on Sando's face, Katalie elaborated. "That was until my chief father married his widowed mother."

Katalie explained that her and Renard Blackwind had been friends when they were young until Renard and his family moved to another village and they lost touch. When they next saw each other, it was at her mother's funeral where they were now eighteen years old and romance blossomed. Unfortunately, a romance also blossomed between her father and his mother who had also lost her husband. The latter romance was the one that ended in marriage and thus doomed the former in the eyes of the tribe as they were now brother and sister.

"It was Renard that convinced me to continue our affair and to keep it secret as you see, we'd fallen in love by then," she explained. "Unfortunately, when my father named him as his heir, the idea of all that power went to his head and that's when everything changed. He displayed his power in cruel ways under the guise of endorsing justice. When he began suggesting that he was going to force me to do his bidding unless I wanted the truth about us to be revealed, I'd had enough, and I left and went where I knew he wouldn't find me."

Sando was completely silent, not sure what to make of this. But he knew that he understood now. She hadn't abandoned her people; she'd run away from a mad man who wanted power more than he wanted her. "Katalie, I'm," he struggled to say the word, but he knew what it was. "I'm sorry." Sando had moved in to embrace her but was pleasantly surprised when she kissed him instead.

A moment later she jumped away. "I'm sorry. I'm so sorry, I didn't mean to."

"It's okay." But it was clear that it wasn't because there was an awkwardness that couldn't be talked away. Things had changed between them and he knew it. But he found himself wanting them to change because he couldn't help it: he liked this woman.

As more days passed, Sando got stronger and stronger. However, they'd never spoken about the kiss again. Sando wanted nothing more than to kiss her again, but also didn't want to do something that made her feel uncomfortable, not after what that monster had done. One day, they found themselves seated around the fire again when Katalie finally asked what he was doing so far from his tribe.

"I was on a spirit walk. I was trying to trigger a curse to become a meqa-moya."

"A what?"

"Meqa-moya. It's translates to 'leaps through air'."

"What's that?" When Sando explained what the beast was, she smiled, recognizing the mythology. "I've heard of those. But I thought they were called metamorphers."

Sando rolled his eyes. This was not the first time that he'd heard the butchered version of the name. "You sound like what the foreigners call them. It's meqa-moya."

"Yes, well, they pronounced it like that because they couldn't pronounce me-thwa more-yeah." When Sando laughed, she made a face. "Don't laugh. It's not an easy word to pronounce."

Sando took sympathy on her and showed her how to say it including what her tongue needed to do and how to get around the syllables. Eventually, after many, many failed attempts, she got it.

"Okay," she said, "so why did you want to become a meqa-moya? From what I understand, it's a curse to be one. At least that's how the legends go when they talked about the War of the Claws."

"It's not a curse."

"But even you called it a curse a moment ago."

"That's because it used to be a curse and now it's just called that because no one bothered to find a better word for what this is. But nowadays, it's an extraordinary honor."

"Okay, so why was it a curse and what changed?"

Sando recalled the history he'd been taught. "Back when the foreigners, the Emperians, came to our lands, they went to the Nite Pole and brought Darkness back with them. Now, while most of the Bantu people had tolerated the foreigners on our lands because they claimed that they were only here to mine gold crystals, the Pula tribe had never trusted them from the beginning. So, when they heard about the foreigners bringing this evil into the world, they'd had enough.

"As the wielders of the Bantu people, they had the knowledge and the power to do many supernatural things but instead of using their power on the foreigners, they decided, instead, to punish the royal families of each tribe for allowing the foreigners to come onto our lands in the first place. They conducted the spell and from that day on, every male member of the Pula, Kwacha, Kwanza and Golide royal families – even cousins – were forced to shapeshift into these wolf-like beasts every time the moonlight touched their skins.

"While designed to punish them, there was a beautiful side effect as the Bantu people who'd been cursed, now had the power to rid their country of the foreigners for good. Over time, they would become the protectors of the tribes. They would even go on to ask the Pula wielders to give them female companions and it's believed that the first of the female meqa-moya were actually animals that were turned into humans. That's where the idea of men becoming wolf-like and women becoming cat-like meqa-moya came about.

"Anyway, while the curse was passed down from father to son and daughter, the nature of the curse itself changed as the Pula wielders never intended for sins of the father to be passed onto the son. This is why the children of meqa-moya must trigger the change in order to transform. And that's why we call it 'triggering the curse'."

"So, does that mean every tribesman must go on a spirit walk to become a meqa-moya?"

Sando didn't answer immediately, still disappointed that he hadn't become one yet. "No. There's no science as to how a tribesman becomes meqa-moya but I am the first son of a king to go on a spirit walk in three generations."

"Wow." Katalie could see that he was upset by the idea. "So that means your family members…"

"My brother and sister triggered their curses in a fight while dueling back in the village. I'm the only one that failed to do it."

"Is that why you attacked the bear?"

Sando nodded. "I thought if I cut out its heart that I'd finally transform."

"Why? Why did you think that?"

"Because I had a vision of an ancestor who told me that the heart was the key. Apparently, I'd misunderstood his words."

Katalie caught Sando's tone. "Does that mean you're going to go out there again and try and trigger this gift of yours again?"

Sando nodded. "It's why I'm out here. I can only go back home when I become a man."

"Where will you go?"

Sando shrugged. "Where my spirit takes me."

That wasn't the question Katalie wanted to ask. "When will you go?"

Sando sighed. "Well, I'm all healed up, so I'll probably go as soon as the sun comes up."

Katalie swallowed. It occurred to her that she wasn't ready to let Sando go. "Wow, I don't know what to say."

By Bernard Bayede

Sando knew what she was feeling because he was feeling it too. "Katalie, I have to go. I have to trigger this curse. It's the only way I know my life has meaning with the tribe."

"But your life already has meaning. It had meaning to me." Katalie realized what she'd said and went on. "I mean, I healed you; I fixed you, I cared for you and I didn't do it so that you can go get eaten by a bear."

"Bears don't eat humans," said Sando missing the point.

"Sando, please," she said, asking him not to start. "I'm trying to say that I don't want you to go."

"I have to. This curse is all I have."

"Stop calling it that. It's not a curse. In fact, the only curse here is that part of you that believes you have to do this. Sando, this thing you want is a gift and gifts are not received unless you deserve it."

Sando contemplated this, not knowing how to react. "Are you saying that I don't deserve to be meqa-moya?"

"What I'm saying is that all gifts are bestowed by the will of *The Light* and maybe you're not meant to receive yours yet. Maybe, you're meant to receive something else first."

"Katalie, what are you saying?"

Katalie wondered if he really wasn't getting it. "Sando, I want you stay and I want you to stay because I love you and I think that you feel the same way about me."

Sando struggled to hide his smile at the revelation. "You love me?"

Katalie was unsure how to answer this. "I love you," she simply repeated. "And if you feel any similar kind of way toward me then stay. Stay with me and—" Katalie was suddenly interrupted by a kiss.

The kiss was passionate and loving. Katalie didn't need to be told how Sando felt. She didn't need to hear him say it. She knew that he loved her. And while she didn't know if he would stay with her forever, she was definitely sure that he would stay with her tonight.

When Sando woke up in the very early hours of the next morning, he was surprised to find that he was alone on the blanket that formed his makeshift bed. He'd gone to bed with Katalie in his arms just hours after she told him that she loved him but now he was alone. It was still dark outside. He had a smile on his face thinking about last night but then remembered what he'd dreamt about.

He'd been taken back to the memories of Yetu except this time to his death at the hands of Lady Lakewalker's chief father. Sando had wondered what the dream was supposed to mean when Yetu's words had come to him at the moment of his death. "To obtain the power that you seek, consider the heart and remember that whatever does not break from the cracks can only help to make it stronger. And that strength is the one you seek to be worthy."

Now that he was awake, Sando consciously tried to decipher it as he lay in bed. Was he talking about a broken heart? That explains the first vision of the night he killed Lady Lakewalker. Because he'd given himself the broken heart. But he'd only gotten the broken heart after triggering the curse. *Perhaps it's not about whether the heart is broken just that I use it in order to trigger the curse*, thought Sando. It was certainly possible that that was what he meant about it being stronger from cracks. So, was this all about strength of character; having a good heart; being worthy? *Wait, is that what Katalie was talking about last night: not receiving a gift until you were worthy?*

That was it. It was about his character and so far, he'd been thinking selfishly about becoming meqa-moya rather than thinking about what it was all about: becoming a protector of the tribe. He was supposed to think outwardly if he wanted to trigger it. Excited, Sando got up go to look for Katalie and tell her that he'd figured it out and that he was no longer going to go out there and leave her behind.

He got dressed and walked out of the cave and immediately knew that something wrong. Fortunately, he'd been smart enough to be carrying his indestructible spear so when he walked out to find Katalie on the ground, lying before a stranger, he was prepared.

Sando carefully noted that Katalie was still breathing, meaning that she was merely unconscious but not dead. Only then did he take in this stranger, sizing her up. She had fiery red hair and pale skin, almost as white as stone. She wore a dark silk shirt with a dark dress, and she held a sword in her hand. Judging from the handle design of the handguard, it belonged to one of those Emperian noblemen rather than a soldier. She looked like she knew how to use it.

"What have you done to her?" asked Sando through gritted teeth.

"Who, her?" said the redhead with darting eyes. "Oh nothing. Just a bump on the head. Which is pretty much nothing compared to what I did to her."

The woman stepped aside to reveal another unconscious person behind her. This one was also a woman and from what Sando could see from where he was standing, she looked like a corpse of a beautiful woman. Something told Sando that this woman wasn't dead. While her skin was as white as the snow and her body was as still as a river rock, her blonde hair was as golden as the sun and her lips as red as blood. No, she wasn't dead, but he did wonder why she so still when the redhead explained.

"Have you ever heard of a black crystal?"

Sando showed no surprise. "You're a wielder from Emperia."

The wielder smiled. "Very good. Ember is the name," she said, smug.

"Why are you here?"

"I'm taking a tour."

"Why did you attack Katalie?"

"She refused to be my tour guide."

Sando scoffed. "And let me guess," he said pointing at the slumbered beauty, "she broke your compass."

173

Ember laughed and turned to look at his sleeping blonde companion. The woman was lying on a flat wooden sled with no reigns or animals to pull it. "Oh Dora? No, she killed my brother. And now I'm going to force her to make it up to me."

Somehow these answers only gave Sando more questions. But he needed to ask his first one over again. "Why are you here?"

"I told you. I'm taking a tour. If you want specifics, I'm here to see that place you call the Nite Pole." Ember smiled when Sando's eyes widened. "I see you've heard of the place. Fancy giving me directions?"

"You're not going there. We're done with you foreigners coming here and doing whatever you want. The darkness in that place stays put!" Sando instinctively twirled his spear in a circle before standing in a fighting stance.

Ember smiled again. "Oh dear. I see I've upset you. I don't suppose it would be any consolation to say that my intention is to put something in there and not take something out?" Her words didn't sway him. "I did not think so." She twirled her own sword. "Fair warning, this sword is a hundred-years-old and I killed the man that it belonged to."

Sando wanted to smile but refrained from giving away the nature of his own weapon and instead thought of how he was going to fight with his almost-healed wounds slowing him down. Sando advanced slowly but Ember moved fast. They engaged in a series of moves with Ember swinging fast and hard. Then she lost her smile and pulled away.

"Well, well. It looks like someone has an indestructible weapon. And I was very much looking forward to this duel." Ember swiftly put her sword in its sheath and took something else out of a hidden pocket in her belt. "We'll just do this the old-fashioned way." What she'd produced was a red crystal.

Sando knew immediately what the crystal was and launched himself at Ember only for her to stop him in mid-air with the swing of a hand. "Let me go, wielder!"

"So, you can kill me? I think not. What I think," she said taking a small black crystal out, "is that I'll keep you just like this." She stuffed the black crystal into Sando's mouth. She smiled. "Now stand still, you hear. No moving."

The words angered Sando because he knew as well as she did that telling him to stand still while putting a black crystal on his person was as good as freezing him in ice. Making it sound like a suggestion was only insulting. Sando was forced to watch as Ember pulled Dora's sled with her mind before stopping and contemplating something.

"And just because you caused me such aggravation, I shall leave you a parting gift." Ember then slowly plunged her sword into Katalie's chest with Katalie's eyes widening from the pain.

"NOOO!" Sando screamed the word in his stuffed mouth as he watched Ember kill the woman he loved right in front of his eyes, and being unable to do anything about it. Anger boiled inside of Sando as he watched the life leave Katalie's eyes. It only grew, watching Ember wipe the blood off of her sword as if she'd simply slaughtered a reindeer.

Sando could feel the anger in him, flow through his veins, into his blood. He suddenly felt himself get very hot, not unlike Mlumbi's mark except he felt it across his whole body. Finding his body reacting in a way he'd never felt before, Sando willed himself to move, the black crystal be damned but nothing. Instead, he felt a bone break and then reform. It was painful but Sando didn't care as he knew what was going on. It was happening. It was finally happening!

Ember heard the cracks and her eyes popped open when she realized that they were coming from Sando. "Well, well. What have we here? You're a metamorpher." She looked up at the moon lingering in the sky, contemplating the hours left until daylight. "A moon that big and a crystal that small, it won't be long until you're free, so I think I'll take my leave now."

177

While Ember started away, she used the red crystal to tow the sled with the one she'd called Dora on it and started making her way up the mountain, leaving an angry Sando literally shaking with fury. Sando continued to transform ever so slowly while he watched Katalie's blood stain the snow. He allowed his fury to dull his pain and do the work he needed to be done. He was going to avenger her. He was going to avenge the woman he loved. And he was going to do it by fulfilling his destiny as what they called... a metamorpher.

THE STORY OF
THE BLADESLINGER

Princess Lee had never really had much patience for politics. Perhaps it was the inevitability of it all what with her being the heir to her father's throne. It felt like she was being stripped of her choices which was ironic because everyone else in the Kingdom of Lite Daun believed that kings and queens could do whatever they liked.

However, the painful truth was that there was a trade-off when it came to living the life of a monarchy: you get to rule the kingdom, but you also have to be responsible for it. This meant she didn't get to live wherever she wanted to; nor do whatever she wanted to; nor be with whomever she wanted to. In fact, her father had called these three things 'the forbidden deeds', telling her that when he was but a prince, he'd also abided by these ideals and kept clear of these deeds. Princess Lee had no intention of doing that.

This was the reason that she was currently in the middle of the Ocean of the Rising Sun on a ship the size of which was far beneath a woman of her station with sails that did not belong to her House. She knew that her father would not approve but she needed to know what it was like to be someone without a great destiny. The ship was a simple fishing vessel. But, of course, any vessel from the Kingdom of Daun was not just a vessel. It was made of grand, dark oak coated with melted white crystal, making it indestructible – something of an expense in other places in the world but not on an island nation where it was in abundance.

Princess Lee had stowed away on the ship in secret but not without her loyal protector, the drakana known as Kai Kamakazi. The ancient Order of the Drakana

Sanrai were powerful warriors, knights by another name. Already trained from a young age to be masters of the katana sword, those that survived the training would drink a potion made of lava and melted blue crystal that would do two things: allow them to breathe fire from their mouths on command and for them to grow dragon-armor over their skin.

Like almost everything else used by the drakana, the armor was grown over a drakana's body by having the warrior bathe in waters that pertained essence of lava after they had drunk the potion. Once they emerged from the waters, the armor would have grown and only strengthened over time. Princess Lee herself had never understood the drakana's obsession with dragons and lava as the dragons that roamed the world were long since dead by the time humans inhabited it. Legend had it that a giant rock falling from the stars wiped them out and Princess Lee couldn't understand why any warrior would worship a beast that couldn't survive a rock, however big, falling from the sky. But alas, the obsession with dragons was one passed down from generation to generation.

These warriors answered only to the King which was how Kai was with her now. It had taken some getting used to Kai and the fact and matter was, when he was first assigned to her at the age of thirteen, Princess Lee would frequently sneak out at night. However, Kai would prove himself resourceful and find her every single time. She eventually came to the realization that trying to escape him was futile and instead, simply invited him along. While initially resistant, she managed to convince him by saying that the best way for him to protect her was to come along because there was no way she was going to stop trying to see the world.

This was how he had ended up on this ship, with that grumpy look on his face. She'd gotten used to that look and it now somehow fit with his topknot of long black hair and frown lines that hid that he was only thirty-three, making him twelve years older than her yet looked twenty years her senior.

Princess Lee couldn't stand his silence any longer. "If there's something on your mind," she said in their native tongue, "speak, Kai. I will not have you ruin this perfectly good day out at sea with your persistent frowning."

"We should not be doing this. When the King finds out you're gone."

"My father will not find out, not unless someone tells him, and I trust everyone on this vessel not to." Princess Lee had made a point to only take a half dozen people with her – just enough to man the ship. "Besides, my father believes I have gone to visit my aunt across the great river. He knows better than to expect me back for a few days."

Kai momentarily lost his frown to break into a very subtle smile. "Your Highness, I think you underestimate your father's resourcefulness when it comes to protecting you."

"No, I do not. That is why I have you here. So that he knows beyond a doubt that I am in no danger. It would take weeks before he ever believed that you failed in your duty to protect me."

Kai then rubbed his bearded chin thoughtfully. "Still, I have a bad feeling about this."

Princess Lee rolled her eyes. "You always have a bad feeling about something. Isn't that why you chopped off Pita's ear once?"

"That was eight years ago and if I recall he had tried to touch you without you giving him permission."

"You overreacted."

"I'd only known you a few months then. How was I to know that you were familiar with a boy's touch?"

Princess Lee smiled, not just from the memories of Pita before he left the Capital, but also of Kai's ever serious nature which had caused her to make quite a few apologies back in the day. "Yes, well that's all behind us. But you need to put your bad feelings about everything behind you too, Kai."

Kai simply made a noise under his breath and went back to his watchful demeanor. His eyes always seemed to be watching everyone including their skeleton crew, although Princess Lee wondered why. She'd never be interested in anyone on this ship. Of course, the reverse couldn't be said as the Princess was aware of how beautiful she was. With a light brown complexion, large brown eyes and long black hair tied up into two tails, she was one of the more beautiful women to come out of the Capital.

In her effort to remain below the radar, Princess Lee had decided to dress less feminine and wore a plain brown tunic with matching pants that went with the large farmer's conical hat that was now slung behind her back. Despite the more understated manner of dress, she knew any man would still find her attractive.

Princess Lee watched as Kai continued to look around, his eyes eventually moving out to sea. The Princess rolled her own. *What is he hoping to find?* However, when she looked at him again, she saw his eyes had popped open. Her eyes had barely gotten a chance to follow his when he suddenly shouted.

"MAN OVERBOARD!"

Everything happened quickly after that with two men coming quickly to see what was going on. While the two men argued about whether the man floating in the ocean was one of theirs, Kai – without thinking twice – dived into the water, making a beautiful arc before entering the water with a small circle of a splash. When he surfaced, he was next to the man with his hands around him, preparing to tow him. Princess looked back at the men who were still standing there, looking at the drakana in awe of his heroics.

"Well don't just stand there!" she said, shouting at them. "Get some rope and throw it down to him! Help him!" They didn't need to be told twice as her words were as good as the King's. A few minutes later, Kai and the man were tumbling back onto the deck of the ship. While Kai was out of breath, he was okay, so

Princess Lee attended the man. He was still breathing so he hadn't drowned and was simply unconscious.

It was only now that she took in the man's looks and saw that he had russet brown skin with red cheeks, black hair that curled to a stop around his ears and neck, and stubble on his face. Judging from that, she discerned that he must have been from Tandem Solari. But the clothes he was wearing suggested something else… he was wearing two parts of a three-piece suit.

The suit was black, with black trousers, a black waistcoat and a white shirt but the coat was missing. He was also wearing black leather gloves and black boots with spurs on the back. There was only one thing missing that would confirm what this man was and as if on cue, Kai called out to them.

"Your Highness, you must see this." Kai was leaning back over the side of the ship but turned around to reveal what he'd brought up from the water. It was a black hat with a high crown and wide brim. "You know what this means."

"He's a bladeslinger." Instead of saying the words like this was something bad, Princess Lee was in awe. She'd never met a bladeslinger and honestly believed that she never would and now here he was. Except, she was the only one who felt this way.

"I think you mean *blood*slinger."

The Princess was aware of that expression: a slur against bladeslingers due to the rumored part they played in the Great Arker Fall. It was the reason that they operated in secret in Emperia and were only truly known amongst supernatural beings. So being in the presence of one now was something special... for better or worse.

"Why is he here, out in the ocean?"

"Who knows and who cares?"

Princess Lee hated his tone. "I do. I care, Kai. You should know better than I do how much fate matters to our people. Nothing happens without a reason. All things are by—"

"By the will *The Light*." Kai knew all too well of the saying as it was an important one in the mission statement of the drakana. Kai let what the Princess was saying sink in. "You don't truly mean to allow him to stay, Your Highness?" He knew the answer. "Princess, we should throw him back into the sea. Let him fend for himself."

She ignored him. "We need to find out why he's here."

"We don't need his kind on our ship."

"*My* ship," said Princess Lee, pulling rank. "Don't you forget that.

Kai knew better than to argue that point. He looked at him then back at the Princess with a little more desperation in his eyes. "Your Highness, he's dangerous."

Princess Lee gestured to his clothes. "Look at him, he's not armed. A bladeslinger with no blade. Search those feelings you're forever having, and you'll see that something is out of place here, Kai."

189

It was clear that Kai didn't need to be told that something strange was going on. "So, what is your intent, Your Highness?"

Princess Lee thought for a moment. While she wanted nothing more than to know what this bladeslinger was all about, she was well aware that as a member of the Daunese royal family and daughter of the reigning King, she couldn't afford to expose herself. So, she came up with a plan. "Well the first thing is, don't refer to me as Your Highness."

"What?" said Kai.

"From this moment forth, refer to me as Lady Lee Ohara." Ohara was her mother's name when she was but a maiden. "Do not call me 'Your Highness'." Lee turned from the shocked face of her protector to the other sailors. "That goes for all of you as well! You may call me 'My Lady' or 'Lady Lee' but not Princess or Your Highness. Not until we set off back in the Kingdom of Daun. Is that understood!?"

Unlike Kai, they obeyed immediately. "Yes, my lady."

She smiled and turned back to Kai. "This is my wish so it shall be your command, yes?"

"If your wish if for me to refer to you as something below your station, then yes, I shall obey, of course. But I still do not think that this man—"

"This man is our guest from here on out, Kai. Now please, take him to one of the cabins" He nodded and picked the man up. "And Kai," she said barely looking at him, "I shall like to know when he wakes up."

"Yes, *my lady*."

Lee never liked using her royal authority with Kai, but she also knew that sometimes it was necessary to remind him that he answered to her and his duty to protect her did not afford him the luxury of disobeying her. Fortunately, as a Lady, she was still afforded the luxury of being treated as a noble, so making commands to her people would not betray her rouse.

But her clothes would, meaning that it was time to change.

*

An entire day had gone past by the time the bladeslinger woke up. When Lee walked into his cabin, she was wearing a beautiful, form-fitting dark, red gown that reached below her knees called a keipo with trousers underneath that matched and boots. It was an outfit traditionally but not exclusively worn by the wielders of their nation – who were all female and all-powerful people, able to channel the power of crystals into magnificent supernatural feats. Lee wore it because it was the only functional piece of clothing she could wear that would not take away from the elegance of being a lady.

She was sitting by his bedside when the bladeslinger woke up. "Who are you?" he asked. The man spoke with a strange accent that placed high emphasis on consonants, suggesting he truly was Solari.

"My name is Lady Lee Ohara. But I think the more important question is who are you?"

"My name is Jeff Longhunter." The man looked around, clearly trying to get a bearing on his surroundings. "Where am I?"

"You are on my ship in the middle of the Ocean of the Rising Sun. Care to tell me how you got here?"

Unfortunately, Jeff seemed confused and too in denial to answer that. "No, no, no. I was on a ship in the middle of the Twilight Ocean." He tried to recall the last thing he remembered. "The ship was attacked. No." He thought hard and then something dawned on him and by the look in his eye, it was something dark. "The ship I was *on* attacked another."

"Why would it do that?"

Jeff sighed. "Because it was a pirate ship."

Lady Lee stood up, trying hard to hide her surprise and feeling of danger. "You're a pirate."

He shook his head fast. "No, no, no. I'm a bladeslinger." He saw that she needed more convincing. "I swear." She still wasn't convinced. "The reason I was on that ship was because I needed to travel in secret."

"Why?"

"Because I was not given permission to go after the," he struggled with his last word, "*person* I'm going after."

"Why?"

"It's difficult to explain."

"Well try. Start with what this mission of yours is and why you should not be on it and end with how you ended up in the middle of the ocean…"

"…without my blades it would appear," he said, unnecessarily finishing off her sentence. He looked at her eying him suspiciously. "You don't have to worry. I don't hunt human beings. But I do have to ask whether you took my weapons. They're holstered in my coat, but I can't seem to see that here."

"When we found you, you were without a coat and without a weapon." She noticed his feel for something in his belt before giving her a questionable look. "I swear, we took nothing of yours."

His mouth creased into a beautiful smirk. "I believe you."

"Good. Now, your tale."

"Right. Well, I'd first have to start with my profession—"

"You're a bladeslinger. You hunt supernatural monsters, yes?"

Jeff looked at her curiously. "Yes. How did you know that?"

"The stories about bladeslingers are legendary across the world. While Emperia may deny that you exist, I know enough of the stories to know a bladeslinger when I see one."

Jeff let out a small laugh. "So much for us being good at keeping secrets. I mean, I know most of

Hellepoint City is aware of us but that's simply because the place is infested with vyrens and we appear more often to put them down but being recognized outside of Emperia, well that's—"

"I'm sorry," said Lee. "Did you say vyrens?" he confirmed this. "What are vyrens?"

Jeff gave her another amused look. "Huh. It would appear that those creatures are better at keeping secrets than we are," he said mostly to himself before answering Lee's questions. "Vyrens are undead supernatural beings that feed on the blood of us poor humans in order to survive."

Lee was horrified. "Demons?"

"We're unclear on that," said Jeff light-heartedly. "Our earliest records suggest that the first of their kind was created by a wielder making creative use of crystals and pure darkness."

"Pure darkness? As in, from *the* Darkness, the entity from the Underworld?"

"One in the same. But we'll circle back to that towards the end of my story. Anyway, we consider vyrens our mortal enemies. They're the ones we're more commonly called out to hunt down and bring them in dead or alive. Most of them end up dead and I can't blame them, considering the alternative is life imprisonment."

"Wait. You're moving too fast. You say that vyrens are your mortal enemy. But if a wielder created them—"

"Darkwielder. It's quite important that you differentiate between your average wielder and a darkwielder."

"A darkwielder. I presume those are the ones that channel their power from the Darkness, rather than *The Light*."

"That's correct."

Lee found herself relieved because a part of her wondered if he would see what she was wearing and presume that she was a wielder and attack her. Of course, she'd never heard of a darkwielder coming out of the Kingdom of Daun and her fear was dependent on his answer to the question she had for him. "So, wouldn't wielders, or darkwielders as you say, be your mortal enemies?"

He shook his head. "No. While we do hunt down and arrest darkwielders, they are far and few between and all the other wielders are in service to the Kingdom so they're not a threat."

Lee hid a dirty look from him. She'd heard of the term 'into service' before and disliked the concept completely as it sounded like wielders were glorified slaves. In the Kingdom of Daun, wielders lived as others did, free to be whatever they wanted. "So, you mostly hunt vyrens then."

"Mostly, but there are plenty of occasions where we hunt other creatures too, like wights and phantoms – all of which are derivatives of vyrens anyway. But, if it goes bump in the night or is supernatural, we are here to serve."

"And how about arkers?" Lee's question stunned Jeff to silence. She wondered if she'd hit a nerve, but she had to know if there was truth to them playing a part in the Great Arker Fall. "Did bladeslingers ever hunt arkers? I understand that they had supernatural abilities too."

"You'd uhm," he said losing his light-hearted tone. "You'd have to ask an Elder about that one. I only know rumors which it appears you know too."

Lee could see it was a sore spot and immediately shifted the subject. "An Elder? What are those, older bladeslingers?"

Jeff laughed. "Well they definitely are older just don't tell them that. The word Elder is a title of the highest rank. Whenever you see a man's name with the letters ee-ar in front of their name, know that they're master edgemen."

Thinking back, Lee recalled one letter addressed to her father she'd found among many in the castle which was written by someone named Er. Quintin Maxwell.

It hadn't dawned on her until right this minute that he was a bladeslinger. "So then, what rank are you?"

"Brother. It's the most common rank you'll find which makes sense considering that we are the Brotherhood of Bladeslingers. The title is denoted with a bee-ar."

Hmm, thought Lee. *So, it would be Br. Jeff Longhunter.* She found that the expression suited him.

"Then, of course, there are the apprentice bladeslingers called Learners."

"Let me guess," said Lee. "El-ar?" *That would have made him Lr. Jeff Longhunter when he was younger.*

"You have it. Now that you know what I do and how it works, we can move on to just what in lloomis I'm doing all the way out here. It all started with our assignment to track down this hundred-year-old vyren."

"Our?" So, he wasn't alone.

There was a sadness that swept across his face. "Yes. My partner and the man who taught me how to do this job. He recruited me; he trained me; and he made me into who I am. He's the reason I get to put a bee-ar in front of my name instead of an el-ar. His name was Brother Konrad Connors."

"And where is he?"

"He'd dead, courtesy of the darkwielder I'm chasing." There was an anger in his eyes. "But it didn't start with her. It started with the century old Theodora Lange."

*

"We arrived at the house under the cover of night on horseback. The house – or what was left of it – was on a manor and had allegedly been burnt down almost a hundred years ago yet there were rumors that there was in fact someone staying in the house, in the cellars below the surface. Since the property belonged to a Lord and Count of Hellepoint whose son in law had been hung as a darkwielder and whose daughter had mysteriously disappeared, we had deduced that she must have turned into a vyren and continued living on the grounds.

"Understand, they'd already been whisperings about a beautiful but deathly looking blonde woman haunting the valley with everywhere she went being accompanied by disappearances and deaths, so there was precedent for the deduction. Of course, we were open-minded to believing that it could have been the Lord himself or even the darkwielder who'd been hung, back from the dead.

"However, when we got there, we found our suspicions validated when we found a beautiful blonde woman, sitting there as still as a tomb. While she was indeed, deathly pale, she did not look like the corpse she was made out to be. Brother Konrad had said it was because she'd been feeding regularly which allows vyrens to look more human than they are.

"After a short fight, we managed to wound her with an iron blade and then contain her with iron shackles.

Iron, you see, weakens vyrens in various ways depending on how it is used. If a vyren is stabbed with iron, it bleeds and feels pain. If it is imprisoned in a cell made of iron bars, it cannot escape even with the strength of ten men. And if a vyren ingests iron, it is like poison and weakens them to become almost sickly. But, of course, iron cannot kill them. A vyren always heals from an attack from iron, no matter how long it takes. Even stabbing a vyren in the heart with an iron blade will not kill it. Only a dagger made of human bone to the heart can kill a vyren.

"Now, while our arrest of Theodora went off swimmingly, what came after was devastating. When we reached the surface with our prisoner, we were confronted by a redhead woman holding a sword. She demanded our prisoner. Theodora recognized her and called her by name: Ember. Although she was aghast at how she did not look a day older than when she was human. This immediately made Brother Konrad and I take her as a threat, believing her to be a vyren as well. Unfortunately, we were wrong. Dead wrong.

"Ember was not a vyren at all but rather a darkwielder which we found out immediately when she froze me in mid-stride and threw Konrad clear across the air. She then took possession of Theodora, placing a black crystal down her corset but not before knocking me out. Or at least, trying to knock me out. Fortunately, I was just awake enough to make out the few words she said to the now slumbered Theodora. She said that she had finally found the power to bring her brother back from the dead and that involved sending a powerful vessel down the mouth of the Nite Pole and that that vessel would be her.

"Unfortunately, before she could take off, Konrad had awoken and engaged Ember in combat. He had the upper hand but Ember was just too powerful and swatted him away once again only this time, instead of sending him flying into the distance, she sent him flying into an explosion of light and he disappeared. She'd killed him."

Lady Lee had been listening to Jeff's every word and could feel the emotion that he was going through and the loss that was weighing on him. "What happened after that? Did you catch this darkwielder?"

He shook his head. "No. What I *did* manage to do was get her full name: Ember Wright, sister of Oswald Wright – a disgraced Lord and confirmed darkwielder. Unfortunately, I was unable to convince the council that she was who I said she was because, according to the information they had, Ember Wright was a suspected darkwielder in the early 700s and with no proof or sightings of a redhead vyren reported, there was no reason to believe she was a vyren and thus no reason to believe that she could look how I said she looked. They declined to let me go after her."

Lee was taken aback. "But" she said, struggling to find the words, "but you saw her. You saw her with your own eyes; you fought her *and* you heard where she was going. I don't understand. Why not let you go after her?"

"They have their reasons and most of them have to do with the fact that they don't trust me."

"Why don't they trust you?"

This was clearly another one of those sore points as Jeff's facial features hardened from the question. "That's a story for another time. The story that you want to hear involves me defying their orders and stowing away on a pirate ship. It had to be a pirate ship as it was the only one that managed to skate under the radar of the red coats and the last place that the other bladeslingers would look for me. But if I'd known what was on that ship, I would have burnt it to the ground rather than board it."

"Why? What was on it?"

"Another vyren. In fact, I think the vyren was the captain and the man I'd believed to be the Captain until then, was a man under the vyren's control. The vyren in question is legendary and goes by the name Dravid Raken. By the time I figured that out, it was too late. It happened when the pirate ship attacked a trading ship heading from Tandem Solaris to Emperia. When I tried to help, I found myself standing across from the centuries-old legend himself and I'm ashamed to admit that I was severely outmatched."

"What made this guy more a legend than any other vyren like Theodora?"

"Because he'd killed bladeslingers," he said with reverence, "which is an impressive thing to do. It's said that he drinks from their blood, which due to the potion that makes us special coursing through our blood, somehow made him even more powerful."

"If he's so good at killing bladeslingers, then how are you here right now?"

"The reason is something I barely believe myself. I was dueling that creature in my losing effort and on the verge of being dealt a fatal blow when, out of nowhere, this wisp of golden light starts moving through the ship. It was throwing pirates left and right and saving many of the lives of the men on the other ship. It saved my life when it threw me overboard."

"A wisp of light?" *It can't be. He can't be talking about...* "You're not suggesting—"

"That there was an arker on that other ship? I barely believe it myself. I mean, all the arkers are dead. Like I said before, I've heard all the rumors about the Great Arker Fall and for the life of me, I don't know how to explain it but what happened is exactly what people have explained in the annals of history as what happened when they were saved by an arker."

Lady Lee had been forced to sit back down from hearing his news. What he was suggesting was impossible. He was suggesting that there was an arker who survived the Fall and had somehow saved Jeff's life. No, it was too impossible to believe. Today, only one legend would come to life. She brought herself back to her senses. "So that's why you're out here? You're chasing Ember Wright who's on her way to the Nite Pole."

Jeff affirmed this. "I need to get to Noctovia and I need to catch up to Ember before she throws Theodora's body down that void and risks bringing back some kind of creature that cannot be defeated."

Lee understood now. She understood his mission. But she also understood something else: their fate. If what he was saying was even remotely true about the arker, then it meant that his mission was blessed from the *Light* above. It was a holy crusade and he'd been brought to her for a reason. She made her decision. "I will help you."

"What?" he said, confused.

"I will take you to KwaBantu ka Noctovia on this ship so that you can stop Ember and avenge your mentor." She gave him a warm smile.

Jeff smiled back. "Thank you, my lady."

*

Another day had passed since they'd adjusted course for the snow-ridden nation of the Bantu people. When Lady Lee had told Kai about the change of plans to help Jeff, he had not been amused and had protested loudly. It wasn't until she offered him a lifeboat to go home that he shut up and accepted the hand that fate had dealt him. Regardless of his choice to remain by her side, Kai had continued to give Jeff hard looks after he'd come to the surface.

Being something of a confident man himself – one who didn't take too many things too seriously – Jeff had noticed and had had about enough of not knowing what quarrel the drakana had with him. So when the lady had finally left them alone, he spoke his mind.

"So, are you going to explain what your problem is with me or are you just going to keep staring at me?" Jeff could tell that he was pretending not to understand. "I know you can understand me. I've run into your kind before in Emperia, escorting your King to meet mine. I know your King makes a point for you to know my language." Jeff had purposefully pointed his finger in Kai's face, forcing him to swat it away with his pride. Jeff laughed. "I don't think you're a nice person, you know that."

"And you, are an insult to your people." Kai spoke the words in Emperian but in a very heavy accent, clearly hating the taste of the foreign tongue in his mouth.

"My people?" said Jeff, amused by the expression. "And what do you know of my people?"

"You are Solari, are you not?"

The words had stung Jeff, but he'd heard them before, so they did not cripple him even in the slightest. "I was born in Tandem Solari, yes."

"Yet you are a bladeslinger."

"Yes, and what's it to you?"

"You disgraced your people by becoming like a foreigner. You dress like them and you invade like them."

Jeff's jaw clenched instinctively before he decided he wasn't going to be a victim in this verbal bashing. "Well, it's better than dressing like you." Jeff gestured to Kai's armor, to the matte, blood-red scales. "Word is that you never truly take that armor off unless injured or retired. So, tell me, how do you relieve yourself in that thing?"

While expecting it, Jeff was surprised by how lightning-fast Kai managed to pull his katana out. He'd swung the curved weapon directly at Jeff's head only to be blocked by Jeff's knife. Jeff watched Kai's eyes as he was equally amazed by how he'd blocked the sword seemingly with his bare forearm. It was only by inspecting the blow that he saw Jeff's blade held in a reverse grip on the inside of his wrist.

"You're armed," Kai noted.

"And you're observant." When Kai disengaged the strike, Jeff pulled out another knife. When Jeff had woken up and saw that his coat – and all his smaller throwing blades in it – was missing, he'd checked his person, assuming they'd taken his other blades only to find that they hadn't. The second knife he pulled out was a twin of the first and what all bladeslingers used in close quarter fights. They were distinguished from all the other smaller blades which were solely for throwing.

The fight wasn't a fast paced one at all but rather one of force and power. They weren't trying to kill each other but rather attempting to display strength. Kai swung expertly, not wasting a single move, while Jeff exercised patience, drawing Kai in to strike, blocking with one knife and then counter-striking with the other. Admittedly, close quarter fighting was not his strong suit as he preferred to be flinging his blade than cutting or stabbing with it. But it was a necessary skill bladeslingers needed for moments precisely like this one.

Both fighters had smiles on their faces and as the fight went on, the pleasure they found in worthy opponents began to shine, including their arrogance as seen by Kai twirling his sword between strikes and Jeff continuously moving his hands as if dancing. While they were clearly enjoying the fight, their growing hatred for each other was evident, no more so than when Jeff finally managed to cut Kai on the cheek.

213

Kai responded with a fury of strikes, one of which forced Jeff to duck. Kai acted quickly and swung at Jeff's feet, forcing him to sacrifice balance to keep his leg only for Kai to grab Jeff from behind and bring his sword up to his neck, getting the bladeslinger at his mercy.

"You're a traitor to your people, *bloodslinger*."

That word made Jeff seeth. "You don't know *anything* about my people."

"I ought to slit your throat right now for your dishonor. It insults me."

However, before Kai could do a thing, Lady Lee returned. "What is the meaning of this!? Kai, let Jeff go!"

Kai obeyed immediately, but when Jeff fell to his knees, Kai continued to point his sword at him. "He is a disgrace, my lady."

"He is my guest, Kai and you will lower your sword."

This time, Kai did not obey. In fact, he ignored Lady Lee altogether and spoke directly to Jeff. "Why would you turn your back on your people and become this thing that you are?"

Jeff decided to humor him. "You've got it all wrong, drakana. They turned their back on *me*." Upon hearing these words, Lee – intrigued, got Kai to lower his sword with just a look and turned back to Jeff, clearly urging him to explain. "My *mother* was Solari. I am only *half* Solari. My father was from Emperia. He was a Lord in fact. Lord Slater Long. He impregnated my mother during his voyage to the jungles of Tandem Solaris but did not marry her and instead left to return to Emperia. When my mother gave birth to me, I was shunned as a half-breed and exiled from the tribes.

"While my mother did the best she could, trying in earnest to get back in favor with the tribes, I grew up to hate them and became determined to find my father and make him answer for what he did. When I finally managed to get to Emperia by trade ship at the age of thirteen, I discovered that my father was long since dead. And, not wanting to return to a home that turned its back on me, I stayed in Emperia and lived on the streets of Hellepoint City, taking the name Longhunter to honor my mother as well, Andrea Hunter.

"Determined from the very moment I got to the city not to be a poor man, I learnt how to swindle in games of chance and fight to earn money. But it wasn't until I saw a bladeslinger fighting a vyren that I knew what I wanted to be. I eventually won myself an iron knife and started practicing with it. And at the age of sixteen, a man discovered my penchant for using a knife and asked if I wanted to become something special. He was the one that recruited me to be a bladeslinger."

"Konrad Connors," said Lady Lee, remembering.

Jeff nodded and continued. "But I left out something about Brother Konrad. I didn't tell you how the council had denied me the chance to become a bladeslinger and that Konrad had to fight for them to see that I was worthy. And the reason they denied me was because I wasn't from Emperia, not truly. You see, I wasn't just forsaken in my so-called homeland on Tandem Solaris, but in Emperia as well. But it was Brother Konrad who explained that it wasn't simply because I wasn't Emperian that they'd denied me, but because they were afraid of change. But he believed change was necessary for people to grow.

"While I let their resentment against me go and trained under Brother Konrad's guidance to be the best bladeslinger I could be, they continued to not trust me, at least not completely. The council was forever testing me, waiting to see if the little experiment that was 'Learner Jeff Longhunter' would fail." Jeff smiled. "I never did. And I became the best of them.

"So, you see why I care not to honor the part of me that's Solari. It's not because I disgrace them but because—"

"They disgraced you," said Lady Lee, finishing off his thought. "Jeff, I'm so sorry."

"Don't be, my lady. I've found peace in being what I am and in the knowledge that my ways make the world a safer place for people like you."

While it was clear that Kai was somewhat more sympathetic to his past, he still couldn't find it in himself to like Jeff. "Tell that to the arkers. You may not be a traitor to your people, but your kind are still the reason that the arkers are no longer here to truly make this world a better place. They're all dead because of *your* kind."

Jeff looked from Kai to Lady Lee. "You didn't tell him what I saw." She didn't answer. "Well, I understand. I wouldn't believe what I saw on that ship either." Jeff turned back to Kai. "If you want to continue hating me, that's fine, Kai. But you won't stop me from stopping creatures like Ember who hurt people. I don't care how evil you think my kind are, I know what I am and know what I have to do."

Lady Lee, sensing Jeff's anger growing, took his hand. "And I promise to help you in every way I can, Jeff."

Kai saw the hand gesture and the look Lee and Jeff shared and immediately knew that there was affection there. While he already hated the bladeslinger, that anger had now grown. He was truly beginning to hate Br. Jeff Longhunter."

*

Jeff remembered the first time he saw the shoreline of Emperia and remembered how beautiful it looked in comparison with Tandem Solaris, with its buildings, towers and castles forming a magnificent skyline. He'd believed that there was no more beautiful view in the world. But now, as they neared the coast of KwaBantu kaNoctovia, the bladeslinger realized how wrong he'd been.

The coastline had appeared through a cold fog and was white from a combination of snow and ice caps. When the ship got closer, it actually had to navigate its way through a field of floating ice and when it could go no further, the sailors prepared a boat.

As Jeff got on the boat, he saw Lady Lee tell Kai to stay with the ship to his absolute chagrin before getting on the boat herself.

"And where do you think you're going, my lady?"

"With you." When she saw that he was about to argue, she smiled. "You didn't think that I was going to let you leave with my boat, did you?"

Jeff had never appreciated anyone pulling rank on him before, even Brother Konrad, but he had to admit, there was something attractive about Lady Lee's authority in this moment. "You may get cold in such a dress, my lady."

Lee answered this by pulling out a vile of something that glowed like lava. "If we drink this, we'll have all the body warmth we need."

After watching Lee gobble down the small vile, she gave a second vile to Jeff. "And what is this?" Jeff wasn't sure why he was questioning the substance considering that he was without his coat and already freezing even though they were still a couple of miles from the coast.

"It's a potion created by wielders from my homeland." She continued when Jeff proved to still be skeptical. "It's just a mild version of the potion that drakana drink when they pass their initiation."

"Whoa, we're not going to grow dragon scales all over our body, are we?"

Lee let out a delightful laugh. "If only we could be so lucky. No, no scales. No dragon-breath either, in case you were wondering. Just this fiery feeling in our bellies that will keep us warm for about a day which is how long we have to find your fugitive and bring her back to the ship."

Jeff looked at Lee, thinking about her last words. Did she really believe that after everything he'd told her about Ember that he was going to let her live? Of course, there was Theodora Lange to consider whom he *would* simply arrest. Jeff drank the potion and was surprised by how fast it worked. He immediately felt warmer just with what he was wearing.

Lady Lee surprised Jeff by taking his hand and placing it on her face so that he could feel the warmth. "See?"

While the warmth was radiant, Jeff was more taken by the softness of Lee's skin. It was like silk. He shook his head, remembering himself and stepped away. "We're burning daylight. Shall we begin our journey?"

The boat trip was a slow one as they navigated the ice field. Jeff explained to the ever-curious lady that the ice was formed from frozen ocean water and got thicker the closer they got to land. In turn, Lee explained that they were approaching the snowed country from this treacherous side to avoid running into any of the natives. This got Jeff curious.

"Have you been to Noctovia before?"

Lee shook her head. "No, but I have heard the same stories that you have about how foreigners from

Emperia invaded the Bantulands looking to mine treasures from their lands."

Jeff confirmed this with a simple knowing look. "The Great Voyage of 492."

Lee scoffed, amusingly. "The *Great* Voyage. I never understood what was so great about it. If the drakana weren't such good warriors, who knows what you Emperians would have taken from us."

This time, Jeff gave her a less knowing look. "I'd heard that Kessler also made land on the Kingdom of Daun Lite. But no one ever said what exactly happened when he got there. Are you saying that the sailors with him and the drakana got into a fight?"

"It was less of a fight and more the death of dozens of sailors." Lee had spoken the words with a sense of reverence that was spooky. "Your people should have left us alone."

This confused Jeff. "Wait, that can't be right. I understood it to have ended differently. That's how we now have trade between our nations, because our ancestors made a peaceful exchange of goods."

Lee scoffed again. "More like my people discovered the riches off the bodies of your men and realized you were all better to us alive than dead." Lee must have realized how antagonistic she was coming off because she changed her tune. "But that was centuries ago and our little nation has reaped the benefits ever since so I harbor no ill will towards your people," she said before pointing a finger, "as long as they know better than to come to our lands *un*invited."

Jeff now understood her point. "You don't think we should be here." It was more a statement than a question.

"I would hardly have had us use this route if I did."

"Look, my lady, I can assure you that I have no interest in repeating my ancestors' mistakes. I have no love for being in Noctovia."

"That's not what this place is called, by the way."

Jeff knew this one and had to admit his mistake. "I'm sorry. It's just what we call it in Emperia. KwaBantu kaNoctovia is quite a mouthful, you understand."

"I would," she said, not upset, "except that even that name, the mouthful that it is, is not the true name of this place. It's just what your people chose to call it to appease the Bantu people and make it feel like theirs."

It is theirs, Jeff wanted to argue.

Lee continued. "The name of this beautiful place is the Bantulands, Jeff. I think the least we can do, with us invading their lands, is call it by its true name."

Jeff could feel the anguish in Lee's words, realizing the version of the story she must have been told by her people. "The Bantulands. Understood my lady."

As they got closer and closer to the shores of the Bantulands, the ice got thicker and thicker. They could now make out more of the land itself and it was even more beautiful up close than it was before. The first thing that Jeff noticed was there were no trees. On most shores he'd made land on, if there wasn't a harbor or a port then there was usually a thicket of tress just behind the beach. While Jeff was not sure what he expected to find on a snow-ridden land mass, his instinct had been to hide the boat in the thicket.

Instead, there were rock formations that formed something of an edge to the beach with one needing to navigate a short cliff to climb to the land behind the beach. Jeff now had a plan which was almost immediately thwarted when the ice got so thick that they could no longer sail through it leaving them a quarter mile away from the shore. While initially afraid that they would have to abandon their small vessel out there in technically, what was still, the middle of the ocean, Jeff realized that the ice was solid enough to walk on and the boat light enough for them to pull.

It took a great effort, but once they got the boat out of the water and moving along the ice, they managed to get it to the beach and hid it from sight against the small cliff. The two of them then climbed over the short cliff and finally saw the land before of them and the treacherous journey ahead of them.

"Wow," said Lady Lee.

"My sentiments exactly." Out ahead of them, spanning miles, was a white countryside with a hilly terrain. In the distance was a mountain with gorgeous ice caps. The route to the mountains was ridden with valleys, gorges and a collection of slopes. Jeff took out a compass he'd been given by one of the sailors. With no lite-star, they were going to have to rely on it. He turned until the needle pointed to the N at the bottom of the compass. "Alright, it looks like we're going that way."

Lee saw the direction he was pointing at. "Please tell me you are joking." When she saw that he wasn't, she pointed too, but upwards. "You do see the storm that is between us and those mountains, yes?"

"You can still turn back if you'd like, my lady."

"And leave you to die alone in that storm?" She shook her head. "Let's go."

"Speaking of us being alone," he said after a while, "do you want to explain to me why you left Kai on the ship?" She didn't answer. "It's just that I get the feeling that he's supposed to follow you everywhere."

"That's my father's doing, not mine." Lee flinched from the small slip.

"Why, who's your father?"

Lee recovered. "Someone important. Why all the questions, Jeff?"

"I just think that our odds of survival would have been higher if you'd brought the drakana with us."

"Well, there's a reason that I didn't."

"And those reasons are?" She didn't answer again. He smiled, almost laughing. "It is a very long journey to where we're going, my lady. That's a very long time to keep silent."

Lee hesitated before speaking her mind. "Have you ever been with a woman, Jeff?"

Jeff wasn't sure where this was going but he relented. "Yeah, plenty, why?" When Lee's eyebrows rose, Jeff knew he had to elaborate. "It's not my fault, I swear—"

"How could you being with plenty of women not be your fault? What are you, a harlot?"

"No, that's not…" he stuttered. "What I mean by that is that the green gene gives us an overactive libido."

Lee had no idea what that meant. "*What!?*"

"At least that's how the scientists explain it." Jeff thought about a better way of explaining it. "Alright, so the potion that bladeslingers take in order to develop our supernatural agility and coordination has a side-effect. It tends to make us," he searched for the right word, "more aroused by the opposite sex than most other men."

There was that eyebrow again. "Aroused?"

Jeff felt so awkward. "Yes. Please can we change the subject? It isn't exactly our most noble trait. None of us are proud about it."

"On the contrary, it would appear that you bladeslingers are very *proud* by the sounds of it."

"Wow. Bed chamber jokes from a lady. As I live and breathe."

"We do have a sense of humor, Brother Jeff."

Jeff laughed. "You sounded just like Konrad." When her eyebrows narrowed from the comparison. Jeff moved on. "Anyway, why did you ask me how many women I'd been with?"

"Well, my intent was to use your lack of female companionship as evidence as to why you wouldn't know not to pry at a woman when she doesn't feel like talking. But it would appear that you know all too well."

"On the contrary, what I would say I know too well is how to open them up." Jeff knew immediately what that sounded like when Lee's eyes popped so far open with surprise that she stopped, frozen in place. "No, no, no. No pun intended. I wasn't intending any sort of double entendre, I assure you. It just came out wrong."

A moment passed before Lee could move again, shutting her open jaw. "I certainly hope so. Good grief, Jeff."

"All I meant was that women tend to feel like they can speak freely with me. They don't remain as bottled up as you do." Jeff noticed that Lee had moved past her surprise to be almost amused. In fact, she had a smirk on her face. Jeff wasn't sure what he could have possibly said that had gotten her face to do that. Was she impressed with his romantic endeavors? Surely not. This wasn't the sort of thing a lady was impressed with. Those weren't the virtues of a man that ladies sought.

"Well, it would seem that you do have a way with the ladies because I suddenly feel myself compelled to tell you my motives for leaving Kai behind."

Jeff looked at her suspiciously, all the while amused by her change of heart. It was clear that she was a playful one, this one. But he could be playful too. "Do tell."

She continued to smirk at him, remaining as playful as ever. "I wanted to get you alone."

"Is that so?"

"It is. But not for the reasons you're now thinking."

Jeff continued to be playful. "Well of course not. We have only known each other for a day. It would be inappropriate." Jeff had purposefully employed this line of reverse psychology to see her response. And there it was: a look. It was a look of worry and concern as to whether he was being serious. It was a look that only someone who wanted him would give him.

Lee realized the look she'd given Jeff and changed from playful to serious, shifting the subject. "I want to know the world, Jeff. I want to explore it and know the different cultures of the world. And be it as it may, you and your kind are a part of it. The reason I didn't bring

232

Kai along is because I knew that he'd spend the whole trip trying to talk me into turning back. He'd most likely use the first sign of danger to drag me back if he had to."

"And you didn't want him to do that? Why? Is it to ask me about my life because I already told you all about that?"

She shook her head. "No. What little I have left to learn from you will not come from your words," she said before swallowing, "but from watching you fight."

"What?"

"Where I come from, honor is a big part of our culture which is why drakana are treated with such respect. There is high honor in being a warrior. So high, in fact, that I have studied their ways and understand that a fight is not just a means of killing but also a way of expressing oneself. You can learn a lot about a people by seeing how they fight. Defensive, offensive, respectful, tactful, with pride, joy or hatred.

233

You learn everything you need about a person from a fight that they sometimes hide with their words."

Jeff took this in. "So, you came out here to see how I fight? But you saw me fight Kai."

"Kai was human, and I knew that you would never kill him. Not if you knew that it would upset me. But a monster such as Ember. I need to see you fight her and then I'll know what kind of man you are."

Jeff thought about this and realized what she must be driving towards. "My lady, if you mean for me *not* to kill the darkwielder then you might as well turn back because I can give you the answer now. She's going to die."

Lee tried to smile. "I knew from the moment you told me your story that you weren't going to allow her to live. But I said I want to see how you fight her. Whether she dies or not, well, that depends on her, don't you think? I cannot very well stop you from killing her if she tries to kill you."

Jeff didn't know what to say. She came all the way out here to watch him fight? What was he supposed to say to that? "Well, I hope you enjoy the show, my lady. Because the fact and the matter is, we could very well be going to the last one you'll ever see. I aimed to keep you some distance from the fighting when it began. But if you're going to insist on seeing it with your own eyes, then I am not sure I can protect you. But if it's what you want—"

"It is, Jeff."

"Then so be it. Let's go. We should reach the base of the mountain before dark."

*

Lady Lee hadn't been sure that they would be anywhere near the base of the mountain by the time the sun went down. So, she was delightfully surprised seeing the mountain stretched out ahead of them. Now all they had to do was cross over a frozen lake and they'd officially be climbing the mountain. Lee noticed Jeff hesitate and decided to show him that the lake was stable when Jeff suddenly grabbed her arm.

"Don't. Something's wrong."

"What are you—"

He put a finger to his lips. "Look," he said, seemingly pointing at nothing. "The fog. I recognize it. This is what happens whenever there's a vyren in the area."

Lee instinctively wanted to ask if that was possible since vyrens weren't known to exist in the Bantulands when she remembered Jeff's story. "Do you think it's Theodora?" Her question was immediately answered when some*thing* came out of the fog with glowing red eyes.

"That's not Theodora," said Jeff, hiding his shock with awe. "Oh Ember, what have you done?" In front of them, in the middle of the lake was a polar bear standing on its back legs, towering over the fog.

Lee was horrified. While she'd heard about polar bears and always wanted to see one, this one was something else. Its white fur was stained with blood that seemed to have come from a wide sword slash across the sternum. But judging from the wound, there was no way that the bear could have survived the attack. Then it hit her. "Is that," she could barely say it, "is that bear—"

"Dead? Yes. The expression is *un*dead but yes. I believe that Ember has done something quite unthinkable and turned that polar bear—"

"…into a vyren!?" said Lee, completely shocked.

Jeff thought for a moment. "More likely a wight." Jeff saw the look on Lee's face and elaborated. "To become a vyren, a human has to be bitten by a vyren and then drink their blood so they have both vyren venom and vyren blood in their system when they die. A wight on the other hand is created when a human – or bear as it so happens – dies with only venom inside them. The difference between the creatures that wake from the dead is that vyrens retain their intelligence while wights become mindless monsters."

Lee looked at the polar bear. It was clearly mindless. "So, this thing would be the latter."

Jeff took a deep breath. "Yep." He then sighed as if contemplating his fate. "Stay here for a minute, my lady," he said stepping onto the ice.

"Where are *you* going?"

Jeff was once again playful. "Oh, not too far. I just thought I'd be polite and introduce myself."

"You're not really going out there are you?" No answer. "You can't fight that thing. That thing will kill you."

"Only if I get too close," he said pulling out his iron-bladed knife. "But what I have in mind," he said flipping the knife so that he was holding it by the blade, "won't require quite so close an introduction."

"What are you going to do?" Lee watched as Jeff took an elaborate stance and raised his knife with his far hand, getting ready to throw it. "You can't be serious."

"It's not exactly my best plan. I mean, this knife isn't even weighted properly so there's a good chance I'll miss the bear completely let alone hit it directly in the heart." He then smiled a cocky smile. "And yet…" Without any more pomp and circumstance, Jeff threw the knife.

Lee flinched, expecting Jeff to do nothing but lose his knife, but was shocked when Jeff's knife not only managed to hit the bear, but also appeared to hit the bear right in the heart. Lee expected the bear to simply collapse to its death but instead the bear didn't even flinch. It simply turned its head towards them and started advancing.

"Damn," said Jeff, still playful.

"Damn!?"

"I was a little off. Missed by inches by the looks of it."

Why was he waddling off about this *now*? "Whatever, Jeff! What now!? That thing is coming!"

Jeff answered by pulling out his other knife. "Time for plan bee." Before Lee could get an answer, Jeff ran onto the ice in a different direction to the bear so that the bear was forced to turn towards him and away from her. She watched as the bear advanced and couldn't help but notice that it wasn't nearly as fast or as fierce as it should have been. Clearly that vyren venom didn't undo the effects of being dead.

Jeff watched as he used his supernatural agility to move around the bear. Remembering what she was taught about fights and what she'd said to Jeff earlier. She saw that Jeff was being smart and staying away from the bear's wild swinging arms but barely managing to do any damage with his superficial cuts. He needed to get closer so he could stab it.

As if reading her mind, Jeff ducked one last strike before moving in for the kill and plunged his knife right next to his first knife, in the chest of the bear. But the bear barely flinched and instead grabbed Jeff around the throat and lifted him. Ever resourceful, Jeff held onto both his knives and managed to pull them out, adjusted his grip on both weapons and thrust multiple times into its shoulders. The bear finally let go and Jeff crumbled to the floor, coughing.

Lee realized that Jeff was helpless. She was about to go onto the ice to rescue him when something raced past her. It wasn't until she gave it a closer look that she realized that it wasn't an it at all, but a person dressed in dragon scale armor. It was Kai. *What is he doing here!?*

Again, Lee's question was answered when Kai took out his sword and charged at the bear. With one stroke of his sword, Kai chopped off the head of the bear just as it reached down to kill Jeff, saving his life in the process. Lee made her way across the ice and checked on Jeff.

"Are you okay?"

Jeff nodded. "Thanks to your valiant protector."

Lee turned to Kai. A moment ago, she'd been eager to rip him a new one about disobeying her order but now couldn't find the heart to scold him. "I see you found us alright. How long had you been following us?"

"Long enough Your Highness."

Lee flinched hearing Kai call her by her true title. She turned to see Jeff's astonished face.

"You're a princess."

Lee wanted to say that she could explain but knew better than to insult him like that. "I didn't want you to treat me like a princess."

Jeff was back on his feet. "And treating you like a noblewoman is somehow different?"

"They're subtleties. For one, you have the balls to flirt with me when you thought me just a lady. Would you have done the same if you knew I was a princess?"

Jeff shrugged. "Maybe?" Kai took a notable step forward.

"Really? The daughter of the King and future ruler of Daun Lite? You would have had attempted to court her?"

Jeff looked at Kai when he answered. "Well, when you put it like that…" Kai stepped back.

Lee was satisfied that she'd made her point. "If I'd made my true heritage known, we may have never had any honest conversations."

Despite Kai standing between them, Jeff risked a step forward, now almost on top of him. "I think you underestimate my ability to be open with a woman. But I understand your reasons. And I'll also understand if you want to go back." She threw a look at Kai. "I'm sure Kamakaze here will help you turn back."

"I'm not going back." Lee turned to Kai. "If you're so determined to protect me, then you will have no choice than to come with us."

Kai looked barely obedient. "That is the way it should have been from the beginning."

Before they started their ascent, Jeff commented on the bear's head, wondering what happened to its right eye. Lee had to admit that it was strange that the eye was missing. It was almost as if the bear had been in a fight recently. *Why would Ember mutilate the damn animal and not just fatally wound it and get it over with?*

The journey up the mountain was surprisingly easier than their journey across the countryside. This was because they were following in someone's footsteps. While they naturally assumed them to be Ember's, Lee noticed that there were sled tracks too along with hoof marks from multiple animals. Was Ember using a sleigh towed by antelope?

They walked through the night, not eager to stop and make camp. But, with there being three of them and each having supernatural body warmth to keep them from freezing to death, there was no need to stop for shelter. It was the very early hours of the morning when they finally saw some sign of life. However, it wasn't Ember they found.

After walking over a small ridge, they came across a body lying on the snow. It was a young woman –

Solari by the looks of it – and she was dead. She'd been stabbed through the heart with a sword and her blood was staining the snow beneath her.

"Was this Ember?" asked Lee, saddened by the darkwielder's killing spree.

"Most likely," said Jeff.

"Do you think she turned her into a wight too?"

"No," said Jeff, definitively. "She's dead. The undead tend not to bleed so much when in transition. This woman bled to death."

Lee's heart wanted to break. "Why did Ember do this?"

Jeff was about to answer when something else caught his attention. He was looking at Kai who was up ahead. "Oh my good Light." Jeff started towards Kai and Lee realized that it wasn't Kai that got his attention but what Kai was staring at. "It looks like Ember did more than just this."

Lee followed after them and, just a few steps away, right in front of a cave, was a man, suspended in place. Except that he wasn't a man at all, not completely. He appeared to be in the middle of a transformation. And while Lee wasn't sure, she swore that the beast that was becoming right in front of her eyes was a familiar one.

"Is that—?"

"A metamorpher, yes." said Jeff. "Or, more specifically, a man slowly turning into a metamorpher."

Kai, who'd taken out his sword, pointed it to the moon, which still loomed in the early morning sky. "It's turning because of the moonlight."

"Okay," said Lee, "but why is he frozen in place and taking so long to turn?"

This time Jeff explained. "It's the power of a black crystal. Ember must have placed one on him when she came through here, killed the girl and then moved on to the Nite Pole."

"Okay, so what do we do?" asked Lee. "Find the crystal and remove it?"

"Bad idea," said Jeff. "Removing that crystal will only allow him to complete his transformation faster. We best just leave him here and keep going." Just then they heard a growl as the metamorpher opened its mouth to reveal large canine teeth. "Before it's too late. His transformation is almost complete."

"We will not make it if we run," said Kai lifting his sword. "You two go on. I shall buy you some time."

"What? Kai, no," said Lee. "Come with us."

"Not this time, Your Highness. It would appear that your fate lies on a different path than mine. It's my job to protect you and staying here to fend off the beast while you two complete the mission is me doing just that. So, please, Princess, go before it is too late."

Lee knew the moment that Kai spoke of fate that theirs was sealed. There would be no changing his mind. If Kai believed that staying behind was him fulfilling his honorable duty, then that's what he would do. Jeff took her hand, eager to get her away from the canine beast. But Lee resisted.

"Go!" said Kai, shouting at Lee for the first time in their lives.

Jeff complimented Kai. "Come, my lady," said Jeff, using her false courtesy.

As they took off running, Lee called back to Kai. "Kai! Try to stay alive."

"Yes, Your Highness."

Lee took one final look at her protector before turning and following Jeff as they disappeared from view. Lee didn't know if she'd ever see Kai again, but she hoped so. She hoped she could see him again even if it was to tell him that she'd behave better from now on. But she knew in her heart that this was likely the last time she was going to see him.

*

They were running now, and Lee was unsure why. Was it because they were running from the metamorpher or because they were running towards the darkwielder? Either way, there was now danger in every direction and simply turning back was no longer an option. But she still needed to know what the plan was.

"So, when we catch up to Ember," she said as they clambered towards the peak of the summit of the mountain, "what exactly are you going to do?"

"Kill her," said Jeff, as if it were obvious.

"Well, I meant about a way of doing that."

Before Jeff could answer, the two reached the summit of the mountain and shock overtook them. Before them, at the base of the other side of the mountain… was no base. Instead, it was an eternal void. It was covered in smoke and there was a feint glow of red and orange that seemed to be coming from deep beneath the world. It was definitely awe-inspiring and it was also so obviously evil. What could the Emperian foreigners from three hundred years ago have wanted from a place like this?

"Look," said Jeff, pointing halfway down the mountain. "There she is!" Jeff was already running down what little path there was.

"I see her. Jeff, wait!" He didn't stop so Lee chased after him. She looked much further ahead of Ember and saw where she was going. As the mountain continued down, it became rockier and rockier; rocks which became darker and darker, looking almost like coal. Ember was aiming for a beautiful flat cliff top sitting right at the edge the precipice.

Still doubting the plan, Lee followed Jeff and noticed that they were gaining on Ember. Lee noticed that it was because she appeared to be towing something on a sled. Looking more carefully, Lee saw that she was actually towing a person, but not a human being. She was towing a vyren. Theodora Lange. And she didn't appear to have a rope to tow her with. Regardless, the weight of her captive was slowing her down.

It took almost an hour for them to close the gap to about half a mile but by the time they did, Ember had reached the cliff top. In order to catch up, Jeff had led them down a slightly different path which had them head towards a cliff-faced terrace that ended just above the cliff top. When they reached it, now above the cliff, they stopped. It appeared that now it was time to formulate a plan.

Jeff pulled out one of his knives. "Okay, here's what we're going to do. I'm going to engage Ember. What I want you to do is secure Theodora."

"What?"

"Under no circumstances are you to remove the black crystal on her person. If you do, you will undo the slumber curse and double our problems."

"Okay. Not to dwell on your parade or focus on the elephant in the room—"

"You know, I've never understood that term. How would one not notice an elephant in the room?"

Lee ignored him. "—but how are you going to engage a darkwielder who is clearly in possession of a red crystal meaning that she can move things with her mind."

"I'm familiar with how the crystals work but I think that won't be a problem," he said pointing to Ember. Below them, Ember was kneeling on the edge of the cliff, overlooking the precipice. One by one, she tossed half a dozen crystals of various colors in her possession into the void before reciting some kind of spell.

"I stand here in the dark, kneeling to its majesty as its servant and I present tribute. Here I am, cast in shadows to ask for the power to conjure from death a fellow servant of the Darkness."

Lee looked at her as she continued. "What is that a spell?"

Jeff shrugged. "Well spells are said to be nothing more than prayers to the Darkness. They are no more powerful than the prayers to *The Light*."

Lee was about to rebut that those prayers used to be answered back in the day by arkers making them very much more powerful when her point was made by a mighty roar emitting from the void. The red-orange glow also seemed to grow more powerful.

Jeff noticed. "I believe that's my queue. Please don't forget yours." Without another word, Jeff jumped down from the short cliff. Lee watched as Jeff stood up, smirking. "Why hello there, Miss Wright," he said as he slowly started forward.

To her credit, Ember did not frighten and did not turn around as she stood up. "Brother Jeff Longhunter. My, my, you are a persistent one."

"I believe you and I have unfinished business." Jeff had lost his smirk. "You killed a friend of mine and now you're going to pay." Jeff was now a few feet in front of Ember. She still had her back to him.

Ember took a very deep breath. "You should turn around and go home, Brother Jeff."

"Don't call me that—"

"You don't want a part of what's about to emerge from that void."

"And what's that? Your brother? Enlighten me, how are you going to change this poor woman into your beloved brother?"

"The Darkness works in mysterious ways. But that's no concern of yours right now. What should concern you is that I will not let anyone stop me, let alone you. Not when I'm this close."

"That's too bad because I'm willing to give my life to stop you. Not in service of *The Light* or out of loyalty to the Brotherhood. But because I mean to see you pay for what you did."

Ember took another breath. "You were warned." As sudden as lightning, Ember turned around and immediately started swinging her sword. This was not what Lee had expected from Ember. Her sword skills were phenomenal as she moved with such grace that it looked like she'd been using the weapon for decades, an impossibility considering her age.

Fortunately, Jeff was no slouch with his much shorter blade – as he'd proven on the ship with Kai – and parried every move made by Ember, However, it appeared that Ember's skills were more than a match, forcing Jeff to pull out his second knife. As Lee watched, she looked for their stories in their fighting styles and marveled at what she saw.

While Jeff moved with fury, clearly with only vengeance on his mind, Ember moved with confidence and a will only born of sheer faith in what she believed in. Lee also noted her sword fighting style. While the weapon of the drakana had them use two hands to duel an opponent, Ember favored the Emperian way of fighting: with one hand. It was how the red coat soldiers fought. But none of them were as skilled as Ember.

Lee remembered that she had a part to play and jumped down from the short cliff and made her way to Theodora. She marveled at her beauty. Her porcelain skin and golden hair was breath-taking even in a slumber. Lee noticed a bulge in Theodora's top and deduced that this was the black crystal keeping her asleep.

Seeing no rope to tow the sled, Lee grabbed the edge of the sled and began to pull. The sled was heavy but, with great effort, she managed to pull it along with hard tugs. Ember noticed what Lee was doing through the corner of her eye and screamed something incomprehensible. Fortunately, Jeff was not willing to let her intervene. He tried to take advantage of the distraction, but Ember was too good.

Unfortunately, Lee's struggles with the sled proved to be a distraction to Jeff and Ember successfully took advantage by punching him in the face and kicking him so hard that he tumbled off the cliff.

"JEFF!" Unfortunately, Lee didn't have time to think about Jeff's fate as Ember didn't waste a single move as she moved towards her, twirling her sword confidently. Lee froze, scared to death. Certain she was about to die, Lee was shocked when Ember suddenly jerked in pain, screaming. Ember turned around and Lee peeked past her to see Jeff, hanging off the cliff, clearly having thrown his knife which was sticking out of Ember's back. "Jeff!"

Jeff climbed back onto the cliff face and spoke to Ember. "Your quarrel is with me, Ember! It's time we finish this." Jeff stood with his knife in hand, his back to the void looking every bit the hero.

Ember, ever the villain, seething at the mouth, twirled her sword again as she advanced. "You want to die first, that's fine with me. Because after I kill you, I'm going to kill her!" The fight began again, this time with it being obvious that Ember was in far greater an advantage.

Realizing that there was no way they could escape their fate, Lee stopped pulling the sled. She realized that this plan was futile and destined to fail unless she changed the rules. She needed to introduce something to this fight to sway the outcome. While it would have been outstanding to have Kai appear out of nowhere and level the playing field; watch him and Jeff work alongside each other in some kind of poetic bookend to their previous prickly relationship; Lee knew this was no more than a dream. However, there was one thing that she could do that would change the game but, unfortunately, there was no way to predict to which end.

However, seeing the losing fight in front of her, Lee made her decision under the hopes that it would be to her and Jeff's benefit and reached down Theodora's top and pulled the black crystal out. Lee immediately felt that she might have made a mistake, but it was too late as she watched the vyren's eyes spring open... and she looked furious, burning with a rage as eternal as her life!

The Night Theodora Died...

THE STORY OF
THE DARKWJELDER

Ember ran as fast as she could from the cemetery, from the city, eager to get away from the very monster that she had created. This had not been the plan. That was what she was thinking as she boarded the ferry that went up the river and away from this forsaken city. She was supposed to be making this journey with her undead brother, Oswald. But that didn't end up happening all because of her... Theodora Lange.

It had been Theodora that betrayed the promise made by her father to marry her brother. It had been Theodora that fell for that Lucas fellow. It had been

Theodora who'd decided to put a giant hole in their plan to put Oswald on the throne and thus set the dominos falling that led to her killing Lucas. It had been Theodora that stood in that courtroom and allowed her brother to be sentenced to hang for her own crime. And when she'd schemed to turn Oswald into a vyren, it had been Theodora that stuck a piece of human bone in him heart and killed him permanently.

That was the reason that Ember had done what she'd done. That was the reason that she'd fed Oswald's vyren blood to Theodora and killed her to start the transition. She wanted Theodora to be damned to an eternal life *without* her beloved so that she could have just a taste of her own agony.

As Ember sat on the boat, contemplating the road ahead of her without her brother, she watched the large paddle wheels working, rotating to provide the vessel the means of moving. They called these kind of boats sternwheelers because of the paddling system but the reason the paddles worked at all was because there was a wielder below deck using a red crystal to keep the paddles turning. Just thinking about this infuriated Ember.

It wasn't bad enough that wielders across the country were being forced to do jobs like this – menial jobs that kept them in a lower class, but it was made so much worse by the fact that most if not all the wielders 'in service' actually liked what they did and believed they were somehow fulfilling a calling. That was the brilliance of the royal government and their manipulation of the only people with true power in the world.

On the surface, the arrangement looked like a quid-pro-quo with the government having a collection of crystals but no ability to use them and wielders having the power to use them but no crystals to do anything about it. Thus, the idea of being 'in service to the crown' began with the government offering wielders not just access to crystals but the means of studying them in special academies. When the wielders graduated, in order to retain access to crystals, they would be drafted into service and posted around the country doing various albeit mundane jobs.

Those jobs could be anywhere from powering an elevator in some random building; to allowing people to communicate through them by yellow crystal; to nursing sick people with green crystals. Some wielders even believed that they'd made it by being involved in constructing bridges, working in mines or forging weapons. They didn't understand that no matter what, they were slaves to the system.

Perhaps the only good thing that the government did on behalf of the wielders was providing education with the academies. Even Oswald understood that when he'd ascended the throne, those had to stay. Without them, there would have been no way for wielders to know the properties of crystals far exceeded their original power when mixed with various elements. Without the academies, no wielder would know that the green healing crystals did different things when mixed with water or fire. Without the academies, no wielder would know that melting a red crystal down and coating an object with it could effectively allow that object to float. No, the academies were the one thing done right in their eyes... but the *only* thing.

This was the reason that Ember and her brother had decided on their plan. They had been fortunate enough to not have been identified as wielders while still children, but they'd still grown up underprivileged, raised by a groundskeeper to a Lord – Theodora's father. It was enough to afford both Ember and Oswald the resolve to want to flip the system on its head. And by the time they were in their twenties, she'd become a Lady and Oswald a Lord meaning they now had the power to do something about the way of things.

The plan had been simple: Oswald would marry Theodora and using her royal blood as a tether and means of becoming King, ascend to the throne and institute a new constitution that saw wielders become the masters of the world. Surely that was the way it should be otherwise why did they have the power they did if not to rule over humans? It was their birth right. But now with Oswald dead, they had nothing.

The ferry came to a stop at a small town called Old Town where, legend had it, the old citadel used to be before it moved to the county furthest lite of Emperia. Now, Citadel City was the closest town to the lite pole. As the ferry docked to let passengers on and off the boat, Ember looked over and noticed a man in a black hat board the ferry. While Ember couldn't be sure, she wondered if he could possibly be here for her.

Unwilling to find out, Ember made her way below deck to hide. She found herself in the baggage deck and decided that if the bladeslinger was here for her, she might as well be armed. It took a few minutes, but she eventually found her bag and the sheathed sword inside. But when she did, someone appeared behind her.

"Oy, whatcha think you're doowun, Miss?" The man had a thick accent.

When Ember turned around, with the sword hidden behind her back, she saw that the man was dirty, covered in filth as if working in the mines all day. "I was just looking for something in my luggage."

"I'm so-ray, but you carnt be down here, yeah. You'll hafta wait til you get off to get ya luggage." He noticed the way she was standing. "Oy, whatcha got behind yor back there, Miss?"

"Nothing that's of your concern. I told you, I was looking for my luggage." The man didn't look convinced at all. "You are not a guard on this boat so why are you asking so many questions?"

The man was offended. "I'll have you know I work, Miss. You see those paddles you see moving the boat? I'm the one that works them, see."

Ember narrowed her eyes, realizing who he must be. "You're a wielder?"

"In your service," he said suddenly proud. So proud in fact, that it disgusted Ember. He noticed. "What? You don't like wielders or sum-in?"

"Oh, the contrary. I have high respect for wielders which is why when I see one that has such little regard for himself, it disturbs me."

"Oy," he said defensively, "I'll have you know I've been working this ferry for ten years now. No complaints. In fact, I've been told by my bosses that I'm one of the best," he said, once again beaming.

"At turning a wheel?" Ember rolled her eyes when the man looked confused by the comment. "Don't you think that your power is worth more than just making a ship move? You should be feared, not made into labor?"

"Why would I want people to be scared of me?"

"Because you're powerful? You're one of the most powerful species in the world. People should be kissing your feet. They should be showing you great honor."

"But being in service of the King is an honor."

"They treat you like slaves."

"Oy, take that back. I'm no slave now, you hear. I'm a hard worker and I'm paid for my work. I get gold crystals every week which I send to my family. Where have you ever heard of slaves having families, hey?"

"You're missing the point. The point is that you could do so much better than this."

"And what would you know of being a wielder, then Miss?"

At that exact moment, there was a giant lurch that seemed to come from directly below them. At first it sounded like a giant animal moving below the ship in the water. But then it began to whisper. "Heeeeeeaarr meeee."

The man, who seemed familiar with the noise, explained. "Oh, that's just the sound of the river. At least that's what I call it."

"The sound of the river?" she said skeptically. "Then why was the river whispering?"

Ember's words changed the man's expression. "You heard that? How could you have heard that

268

unless you're..." Something immediately dawned on him. "Are you a wielder?"

Ember was taken back by this accusation. "Excuse me?"

"Well, while everyone can hear the sound of the river. Only wielders can hear *that* noise." Something else seemed to dawn on the man. "Hang on a moment, if you're a wielder, why ain't you in service?"

"That would be because I'm not a wielder. You just presumed that I was."

"Then how did you hear the whispers I wanda?"

"I don't know. Perhaps it's not just wielders that can hear it."

"Na-ah, Miss. It's just wielders and you're one of us. But if you're no wielder then I could always fetch the edgeman sitting upstairs to sort this out."

It was time to give up the jig. "Alright, you dim-witted oaf. I am a wielder, but I have no interest in being a slave so if it pleases you, I'd like to just be left in peace. So, do me a favor and don't call the bladeslinger."

The man thought about this and seemed to succeed in reaching past his own dim-witted nature. "Wait a minute. You wouldn't be down here hiding from the edgeman, would ya?" Ember's silence spoke volumes. "Ha, a fugitive I see. Well, I won't have no darkwielder doing unthinkable things on this here ferry. So, if it pleases you—"

Ember pulled out the sword and pointed it at the man. "I'm sorry but I can't go back to Hellepoint."

"Okay," said the man lifting his hands, "just put the sword down now, you hear?"

Now with his hands up, Ember noticed the red crystal in his hand. She wondered just how dim-witted this man was and whether she'd get away with her next move. "Give me the crystal?" She saw that it hadn't occurred to him to use the crystal against her. "Give me the crystal of I'll kill you where you stand." The man believed her and gave her the crystal. The moment it was in her hand, the ferry came to a dead stop. Ember ignored this. "How can you carry this around and chose not to do something useful with it?"

"I do something useful. I ferry people from one place to another—"

"That is *not* useful, Sir. I'm talking about changing the world. I'm talking about fighting those that oppose you."

"You sound like a darkwielder."

"Oh, there's no such thing. That's propaganda from the government giving themselves permission to slaughter us. A wielder is a wielder, and you should care when one of us is hunted down by those damned blade-throwing maniacs."

"Hello? Is there a wielder down here I can talk to about getting this ferry moving?" The person speaking was a man, and he was heading their way. Ember acted quickly and pulled the wielder in so that he was now at her mercy, sword to his throat. The stranger came

271

around the corner and revealed himself to be the bladeslinger. "Well, that explains a lot."

"Don't move or I'll kill him."

The edgeman looked at her carefully, measuring her. "Do you know how to use that sword, miss?"

Admittedly, Ember wasn't well versed with the weapon. She'd only just procured it from Lord Edmond's dead body. She sidestepped the question. "I know how to use this," she said, referring to the crystal in her other hand.

This got the bladeslinger's attention. The man was greying at the temples, wrinkles on his face showing an experience that only came with age. "You're a darkwielder." Instinctively, he pulled his coat back to reveal his knife on a belt holster.

"Don't do it. You'll regret it."

"On the contrary. I think I know what I'm doing. For one thing, I know that using a red crystal in a fight requires concentration. And you can't be concentrating that hard if you're also holding a hostage. So, when I do *this*…!" The man had moved so fast that the blade he flung had been but a blur. "…you won't have time to respond."

The blade had come from nowhere and embedded itself in her shoulder. Ember had pulled away in pain, but then quickly flicked a gesture with her crystal hand forcing the bladeslinger to duck out of sight. This gave Ember an opportunity to run. She went all the way back up to the top deck, still holding the sword and swiftly jumped overboard. She stayed below the surface in an effort to make the people on the boat believe she drowned.

While she held her breath, she heard the sound again: the sound of the river. It whispered to her again only this time it was a voice she recognized. "Emmmber." It was Oswald. Ember looked around the river and made sure not to lose her breath when she saw an image of Oswald below her. Ember was sure that she was hallucinating.

When she looked up again, she saw that the bladeslinger on the ferry was searching the water for her, meaning she couldn't go up even for a breath. As the seconds turned into more than a minute, panic began to set in as Ember realized the only way she could truly escape was by not surfacing again until the bladeslinger was gone. Unfortunately, he didn't seem eager to leave. As if turning to him for help, Ember looked down to the image of Oswald and saw him reaching up with his ghostly hand.

Not sure what she had to lose, Ember slowly reached out and she did so instinctively with the hand that still had the red crystal in it. The moment their hands touched, there was a small gush of water that grew from the crystal. At first, Ember thought it was a vortex, but as it formed, she realized that it was a bubble. While the sides of the bubble were unstable, there was no denying that right at the center, was a pocket of air.

Once it grew big enough, Ember stuck her head in the bubble and was relieved to find that she could breateh. She was then taken aback when the ghost of her brother stuck his head into the bubble as well. She was shocked by how real he looked. "You're not him, are you? You're not my brother."

"You already know the answer to that." Something about the way he seemed almost too calm bothered her.

"That means you're a phantom: a supernatural manifestation of the dead."

"Makes sense since I was a wielder."

"That means you're only here because I'm willing you to be here." She didn't need an answer to this. "I'm keeping you from moving on."

"You know the answer to that too."

A sadness came over Ember. "Well go. I don't want to be the reason you can't rest in peace. Go to the Heavens and be done with it."

He continued to remain calm. "And what if I'm predestined for the Underworld? Would you still like me to go?"

What? The Underworld? Only the damned go there. No, her brother was good. He didn't deserve to rot in that place. So why would he say this to her? It occurred to Ember that this could all be in her head and that *she* was the one keeping him here because *she* believed that he'd be condemned to the hells of the Underworld. For all she knew, he was long gone to where he belonged. So, then what was with this ghost?

Ember heard a noise from above and looked up. She could barely see anything through the wall of the bubble which was still unstable like the sides of an actual whirlpool. She looked down to her feet which were still kicking in the water as the bubble only accommodated her head and shoulders.

Oswald's ghost interrupted her thoughts. "Listen to me Ember. I need your help."

"What?" What could her dead brother need her help with?

"I need you to do something important."

"What is it?"

"I need you to bring me back to life."

"What?" Ember didn't know what to say. After all, she'd tried to bring him back after he'd died as a vyren but even that had been about bringing him back undead. What was he asking now? "What are you talking about?"

"I'm talking about you using an ancient type of power that can be used to bring people back from the dead, legitimately."

"And what power is that?"

"The power of the synn."

"The synn?" The synn were a demonic race of beings and the stuff of legend. A legend that had it that they were destroyed in an ancient and final battle between *The Light* and the Darkness in the dimension of Lloomis that was fought between the arkers and the synn. The same legend had it that they were the only beings as naturally powerful as arkers… and they still fell to them. Now people barely believed that they ever existed. "The synn don't exist."

"A rumor well spread by arkers. But the truth is that their power still exists in the ashes of Lloomis, just waiting for someone bold enough to take it and use it."

"I can't get to Lloomis. And even if I could find a gate and pass through it, you're forgetting about the other part of the legend, Oswald. When the synn were defeated, their carcasses were turned into stone for this exact reason: so, no one would dare attempt to use their corpses for themselves."

"They were turned into stone by the arkers to make an example out of them. But the arkers are no more, and their power if there for the taking. And you will not have to travel to Lloomis. Long ago, there were those that saw fit to travel there and bring what they believed at the time to be statues back with them and used those statues to decorate a city."

Ember knew which city he was talking about. It was one of the most famous cities in Emperia with statues sitting on many of the towers said to guard the place from the monsters of the night. Up until this moment, Ember always thought this a myth until now. This explained why there had almost never been a vyren sighting or killing in the city for centuries. "You're talking about Pscycopolis."

Oswald didn't even bother confirming it. Instead, he gave her marching orders. "If you wish to bring me back, you are to go to Pscycopolis and learn how to use this power. Then, when the time comes, you shall bring me back and we can reunite. But first…" Oswald suddenly lifted their crystal-bound hands upward and there was suddenly an explosion of water which exploded upwards.

Ember had suddenly and surprisingly found herself shot upward into the sky before being thrown far across the river where she landed on the bank, coughing up water. She turned towards the river and saw that the ferry had been capsized. There was screaming everywhere. *Did I do this? No, Oz did this… but he's a ghost!* Too aghast to figure out how she'd created this devastation, Ember used the chaos to run away, breaking into a nearby forest but not before picking up Lord Edmond's sword which had landed nearby.

She ran like her life was at jeopardy because it was. If the Brotherhood of the Bladeslingers ever caught up to her, she'd be dead in days. She could never return to Hellepoint City, she knew that. She also knew where she was heading: the city of Pscycopolis. She was going to fulfil her brother's wishes and figure out a way to attain the power she needed. And with any luck, she'd have her brother back by New Annum Day!

*

TWENTY-FIVE YEARS LATER

"Ember. Ember, come here my child." It was still strange to be calling her daughter by a name that was once hers even though it had been a quarter century since she'd last used it herself. While it had all been in an effort to evade the authorities pursuing her and begin anew, she'd found herself unable to truly leave the name behind. So, when she had an opportunity to give birth to the name again when her daughter was born, she did just that.

Her name now was Ashlyn Warlow, wife of Captain Robin Warlow of His Majesty's Navy. Marrying him had not been a coincidence of circumstance but rather a very elaborate plan on the part of Ashlyn. She'd purposely married someone prominent yet not a political leader in order to make sure she didn't move down in class yet also stayed out of the radar of the government. But she also needed someone who wouldn't be around for extended amounts of time so that she could spend all of that time with her daughter.

"Yes mother," said the eighteen-year-old girl. Ember II was a spitting image of Ashlyn when she went by Ember with fiery red hair and powerful blue eyes. While Ashlyn had since dyed her hair black, she still had blue eyes.

"It's time for you lessons my child."

Ember II smiled. "Oh good. I'll go get my journals."

"No," said Ashlyn before Ember II rushed off. "You won't be using your journals today."

"But mother, how am I to know how to use the crystals if I can't read the instructions I journaled down."

"You'll be recalling them from memory from now on." Upon seeing her daughter's face change, Ashlyn continued. "Ember, you're a fully grown woman now which means you'll be going out into the world and you can't afford to be using books when you need to use your power."

"And when exactly will I be able to use my power, mother? Because you promised me long ago that when I became a woman, you would show me what being a wielder really means—"

"And I will."

"When, mother? I thought the whole point of not sending me to one of the academies and having me hide my abilities was so that I'd be free to use my powers at my discretion. But my eighteenth birthday has come and gone, and you still haven't given me the cache of crystals you promised me—"

"You're not ready," said Ashlyn, interrupting her persistent daughter. "You're not ready for what comes next."

"I am ready mother."

Ashlyn knew that Ember II didn't know what she was talking about, but she also knew that telling her wasn't going to cut it. If she was going to prove that her daughter wasn't ready, she was going to have to show her. "Prove it."

Ashlyn and her family lived in a house on the edge of town facing the ocean. While the location was otherwise treacherous during storm season, one of the main reasons that they liked it – other than the fact that it was close to the ocean and Robin's job – was because it had its own private beach. With oceanside cliffs forming something of a boarder on either side of the beach, no one could see into what was essentially a cove which was perfect for their lessons…

Currently, Ashlyn was standing thirty paces from her daughter with a beach fire directly between them and two swords planted in the sand on either side of it. There was a small chest next to Ashlyn, sitting on the sand. Ember II had a similar sized chest on the ground next to her which she was already digging into. Both chests had a collection of assorted crystals that Ashlyn had acquired over the past twenty-five years. While there had only been enough to accommodate one chest when she started teaching Ember II a decade ago, the cache had since doubled as Ashlyn had become wise in how to find them.

"Now before we begin," said Ashlyn loudly so that Ember II could hear her, "do you remember your earliest lesson about the crystals?"

"Do we have to go over this now, mother? Why not get on with the duel and speak of this later?"

"The lesson, Ember!" said Ashlyn, disciplining her daughter. "Do you remember it?"

"Yes. It was about how the crystals came to be. They were formed deep beneath the ground over the course of hundreds if not thousands of years."

"Yes. And where does their power come from?"

"From nature; the world itself. Each crystal and its power have a unique source. Green healing crystals come from a specific tree sap; black slumber crystals are mined alongside coal; yellow crystals of thought are from a specific sand; blue sparking crystals are formed from lightning; red crystals from molten coals and white crystals from the mountains surrounding the Lite Pole."

"You forgot the gold crystals formed in snow."

"I didn't forget them mother. I just neglected to mention them because they don't give wielders any power."

"Yet they are the most important crystal to remember because they remind us that this power doesn't belong to us. It's borrowed. But that doesn't mean they are not still precious regardless. This is my point."

Ember II took a minute to make sense of what her mother was saying. "The crystals have the power, not the wielder."

"Yes," said Ashlyn picking up the only gold crystal in her chest. "Without a crystal, we're nothing but gold crystals: special and precious but otherwise forgotten by those who cannot understand us without that which makes us useful to them. Remember that, Ember, always."

Ember II nodded. "May we duel now?"

Ashlyn nodded. "You remember the rules. The duel starts out with sorcery and ends with weapons. You can use the sea water and bon fire to manipulate the properties of the crystals when you get to the center and first to lose consciousness or yield will lose."

Ember II rolled her eyes. "You explain the rules to me every time, mother."

"Well, this time, you don't have your journal with you to remind you what combining water, fire or sand will do to the power of the crystal."

Ember II rolled her eyes. "It doesn't really matter. My plan is to finish you with your sword," she said eying Lord Edmond's indestructible sword planted next to the more ordinary one by the bon fire. Ashlyn had never told her daughter the true ownership of the sword. "I'm ready when you are, mother."

Ashlyn gave the signal, and the duel began. While Ember II did as she always did and took a black and red crystal in an attempt to freeze her in place, Ashlyn selected a red and blue crystal before starting towards the water. They'd each taken a green crystal, both knowing the value of healing any injuries.

Not moments later, Ember II was firing her power at Ashlyn. Having gotten used to dueling Ember II, Ashlyn had presumed that the first thing her daughter would do would be to try and freeze her in place. However, Ember, showed adaptational prowess when she instead threw her green healing crystal right into the bon fire which caused the fire to leap ten feet into the air as if doused in alcohol.

It appeared that Ember II had remembered something from her journals including how green crystals, when introduced to a flame, became something more powerful called windfire. Ember II acted quickly and used the red crystal's power to control the flames in the air and throw them at Ashlyn.

Ashlyn thought quickly and gestured to the ocean water arriving by wave and lifted it above her head and then brought it down over the flames and Ember II. When she saw that Ember II was soaking wet, Ashlyn placed the green crystal in her mouth as a preventive measure and plunged her other hand with a blue crystal into the water quickly before it returned to sea. She then activated its spark immediately causing her to spasm from the shock that was more commonly associated with lightning strikes.

Fortunately, her almost suicidal plan worked when she saw Ember II also get shocked and collapse. Recovering quickly, thanks to the help of the green crystal, Ashlyn got up and went over to the weapons. But before she could pull out the sword she stopped, unable to move. She realized that Ember II had still been conscious enough to use the red and black crystals to do what Ashlyn had presumed would be her opening move.

Realizing that the size of the red crystal would prevent it from having enough power to hold Ashlyn much longer, Ember II acted quickly and took a cloth and wrapped it around the end of one of the thin burning logs slipping two crystals into the wrapping which now formed a handle. One was a piece she broke off the black crystal – which would keep the log in a suspended state of red-hot. The other was a tiny piece of crystal that Ashlyn didn't remember ever procuring.

Ember II noticed her mother's expression change with the red crystal spell now breaking off. "I found this a few weeks ago. First white crystal we've had in the house for years, yes." Ember II then carefully placed the crystal on the perpetually heated log and watched it melt in streaks around the hot half of the makeshift weapon.

Ashlyn finally broke free and took possession of her sword. "The first white crystal in years and you use it on a stupid piece of wood?" Ashlyn engaged Ember II with anger as they parried moves. Ashlyn was truly annoyed with her daughter, with every move being made of anger.

While Lord Edmond's sword had simply been a keepsake when she took it off his dead body some twenty-five years ago, Ashlyn had since become proficient with it, managing to get her husband to agree to train her in military swordplay. While the

Captain had initially forbidden it, he'd eventually allowed their daughter to learn too which unbeknown to him, was all part of Ashlyn's plan to prepare her daughter. But that was if she survived today's lesson.

After what appeared to be a comeback on Ember's part, the young Warlow eventually found herself at a loss when Ashlyn took advantage of the fact that unlike her mother's sword which was properly coated in melted white crystal, Ember's weapon merely had streaks of the unbreakable material and watched as Ashlyn chopped off the end. With the black crystal no longer attached to the burning wood, it began to cool in the sand. But Ashlyn herself was far from cooling.

Ashlyn kicked Ember II away to get the distance she needed before planting her sword back in the sand nonchalantly and then pulling her red crystal out again and stretched out her hand toward her daughter and began squeezing the air. Ember II immediately felt her airways close and started grabbing at her throat.

"Stop it, mother. You're hurting me."

"Remember when I told you that you weren't ready for what comes next. This is what I meant. To you, this is still a game, but the truth is, it isn't. The truth is, you're going to have to kill someone in order to be ready. Are you ready for that, Ember? Are you ready for that?"

"Ashlyn!" The voice that called out to her came from behind her. It was Captain Warlow. "Let her go, now!"

Ashlyn initially hesitated before eventually relenting. "What are you doing here?" Ashlyn spoke the words unapologetically.

"Apparently, saving our daughter from your madness," he said going to her. "What has come over you?"

"I'm training her, Robin."

He scoffed. "When we agreed that we would not be taking our daughter to the wielder academy and that you would train her yourself, I thought we agreed that she could do it as long as she remained safe. Clearly, this is not safe." She turned to Ember II. "Come along dear."

"No, father. I'm not going anywhere with you." Ember II hated her father, and this was due to the fact that he'd somehow managed to find a way to stand as an obstacle at every turn in her efforts to become a wielder. It was only made worse by the fact that she hardly ever saw him, and he'd become a stranger to her. The hatred was complete with the realization that now that she was a woman, he was going to ship her off to be married to a man she didn't love at his word.

Even now, Captain Robin Warlow showed that he had little sympathy for his daughter's whining. "I don't recall posing that as a question, Ember. You will come with me and as of today, you will not be participating in these lessons. Is that clear?" No answer from Ember. "*That* was a question."

"Yes Captain," she said, remembering all the way back to her first scolding from him and how he'd wanted her to call him by his rank. "It's clear."

"Good. Now come with me." As he dragged Ember II away, he turned to the original Ember. "And you, we'll talk about this later."

*

The woman who now went by the name Ashlyn, knew better than to be the one to bring up the topic. She also knew when the Captain would bring it up himself: at the dinner table. Ashlyn was a little unsettled by seeing that it would just be the two of them and that the Captain had confined Ember II to eat in her chambers.

"You know," he began, "when you revealed to me before we were married that you were a wielder who had no interest in being of service to the King, I thought 'who am I to force her to do what she does not want to'. Make no mistake about it, I thought it was wrong and treasonous to not be in service, but I left it alone because I loved you. When our daughter came of age and you begged me not to reveal her to the government and have *her* in service, I relented, again, because I loved you. But now, after seeing what you did and what you are, I realize that I made a terrib—"

"What I am?" asked Ashlyn, defensively.

"Yes. You're a darkwielder, are you not?"

Ashlyn sighed. "Come on, Robin. That's propaganda and you know it. We've spoken about this."

"Yesterday I may have believed that with all my heart but after today, I realize that there are such things as darkwielders and you're one of them. And I have a mind to call upon the Brotherhood and have them deal with you."

"You wouldn't dare—"

"Wouldn't I?" There was venom in his voice, clearly thinking of doing just that. "Unfortunately, I have no way of knowing whether you'd turn on your own daughter at that stage and have her arrested too."

"I'd never do that, and neither would they. She's just a child—"

"—and the daughter of a darkwielder. Light knows what they would do to her which is why I won't be calling the Brotherhood. But what I will be doing is asking you to leave," he said as Ashlyn began to protest, "and exiling you from ever returning unless you tell me what you are after!"

Ashlyn's complaining came to a dead stop once the Captain completed his ultimatum. "What makes you believe I am after anything?"

"I saw the way you were training her out there, teaching her towards some certain goal. You need her to be ready to do something and I would like to know what that is."

Ashlyn saw that there was no fooling the Captain and she realized that since Ember II was unlikely to be more ready than she is now that their lessons had come to an end, she might as well complete the step in her plan that was inevitable from the get-go. "If you want to know what my plan is, I shall have to start from the beginning which includes letting you know that my true name isn't Ashlyn. My true name is Ember Wright."

Ashlyn explained everything to the Captain all the way until she fled from the riverbank that day, leaving her identity of Ember Wright behind her. She explained how she changed her identity and then immediately began searching for the synn hidden around the city as statues. She explained that while she found the statues easy enough, she'd been hard-pressed to figure out how to gain their power until Oswald came to her again.

"My brother told me that the power of the synn lay in their blood. He told me that in order to understand that power, I would need the blood of a powerful wielder from a strong bloodline. You see, a wielder imbued with generations of knowledge about our power would be powerful enough to conger the knowledge of how to use that power for what I need."

The Captain had listened patiently, bordering on being fascinated with Ashlyn's story. But there was something that confused him. "How would they receive this knowledge? How can you or anyone really determine the means by which to use the power of the synn if all the synn in existence are dead?"

Ashlyn smiled. "Through the Darkness." She saw him shift in his seat, uncomfortable. "You see, the catch to being powerful enough to conger up this knowledge is that the one who will be doing the congering will have to be a darkwielder." She watched, amused, as his eyes lit up from the confirmation and she leaned forward. "Yes, my darling, you were right. There are darkwielders in this world and we belong to a force far more powerful than anything you can imagine. And that force, we serve with loyalty."

"My Light, our daughter. You've been brainwashing her with this doctrine?"

Ashlyn shrugged. "Giving birth to her and training her with my knowledge is the only way I could fulfil my plan to bring my brother back. She will continue my work and her blood will unlock the way."

There was disgust in his eyes. "You'd do all this in the name of your dead brother?"

Ashlyn was insulted. "I'd murder the whole world to have my brother back. My brother was going to save this world but the people that you call noble made certain that that would never happen. And I will *not* stand for that. I will have my brother back so that he can exact his vengeance on all of you."

"You're crazy."

"And you're dead, you just don't know it yet."

"I think I will call the bladeslingers and let them deal with you," he said standing up. "But first, I shall have Ember spirited away. For her own good, I shall have to have her locked up until I can find someone, a true wielder, who can have whatever darkness you put inside her cast out of her."

Ashlyn began to laugh. "Do you really believe it would be that easy? Do you really believe that you can

299

just spirit her away? You don't understand, do you? You've known about wielders, what, the better part of two decades. I've known about it my entire life. That's forty-five years of experience that has stood the test of time. I know everything there is about how *your* kind do things. But you know nothing of me."

"What are you talking about?" He was now truly confused.

"I am talking about the fact that your daughter's hatred of you was not by some happy circumstance," she said, almost too serious, "it was by design. And it was a design that stretches to before you even met me. I specifically chose you because of your duties to the Navy. I specifically chose you because of your misogynistic principles that would have you not only underestimate me but treat your daughter like a possession. I specifically chose you because I knew it would be effortless to drive a wedge between you and her and thus making it easy for her to love me unconditionally."

The Captain didn't understand, neither did he look to try. "Enough of this madness. I am her father, and she will listen to me!"

"No, I won't."

The Captain turned around to see Ember II standing right behind him. "Ember pack your things. We're leaving."

Ember II completely ignored her father. "I think I finally understand what I need to do to be ready."

The Captain still didn't understand but when he saw Ember II holding Ashlyn's indestructible sword, it dawned on him just what was going on. He let out some indiscernible sound, almost pleading just before Ember II stabbed him in the chest. The white crystal coating made the sword simply slice through the Captain's sternum like butter.

As the Captain crumbled to the floor, Ashlyn paid close attention to her daughter and saw that she had no feelings about the fact that she just killed her father. Perfect. That meant that she'd given herself completely to the Darkness in that moment and allowed it to give her the strength she needed. When the moment finally passed, Ember II looked at her.

Ashlyn smiled. "My child, you are ready."

"So, what happens now?"

*

THIRTY-FIVE YEARS LATER

"Now Ember my child, you remember the rules of the duel, yes?" The fifty-three-year-old woman who spoke the words was pretty for a middle-aged woman who still had a whole head of red hair. Unlike her mother, when she'd changed her identity, she'd opted to remain a redhead when she became Cinder Chamberlin. Unlike her mother, she hadn't been afraid to marry a Lord when she married Lord Leonard Chamerblin. And unlike her mother, she wasn't cruel when she taught Ember III the ways of being a wielder.

In fact, it was Ember III who displayed shades of the oldest Ember by taking to the dark far quicker than Cinder did. While Cinder did abide by her mother's teachings and very much was a child of Darkness, she'd found that all the murderous sacrifices that her and her mother had done in the name of unlocking the key to bringing back her dead Uncle Oswald had taken their toll. So, when she gave birth to little Ember the Third, she'd made a decision to at least give Ember III the choice she never had. Alas, Ember III looked to be destined to go to the dark.

"I remember the rules, mother. Now, can we duel?"

Their duel was taking place in a rather large barn on the far side of the estate that they lived on. Taking notes from her childhood, Cinder made sure only to teach her daughter when Lord Chamberlin was away on business like today. The estate stood on the edge of Eden City, overlooking it.

The duel was hard and fast and saw Ember III using dirty tactics but to no avail. However, when Cinder had Ember III at her mercy, she looked into her daughter's eyes and hesitated. Ember took the opening and used her mind to plunge a sharp object into her stomach which immediately made Cinder let go of her daughter and crumble to the floor.

As Cinder lay there, she watched in horror as Ember III simply looked at her, not doing anything. The last thing Cinder saw was Ember III with a disappointed look before everything turned to darkness…

It felt like a lifetime had passed before her eyes opened with a start and as if to mirror the last image she saw, the first thing she saw was Ember III kneeling over her, fiddling with something. Cinder looked down to see Ember rubbing a green paste into her wound. It was from a green crystal. Cinder could also taste something sour in her mouth and realized that Ember III must have also made her drink some green crystal potion which was why she was feeling so much better.

"Sorry about the delay in first aid, mother. But you know the rules: I had to wait for you to pass out."

Was she being serious right now!? "And I supposed me on death's bed wasn't a sign of me yielding."

Ember III gave her an indifferent look. "Helping you before I'd won the duel would have been a sign of weakness, mother."

Cinder knew those words. "Have you been spending time with your grandmother again?"

Ember III didn't answer. "Speaking of Grandma, when is she coming? She sent word that she'd be arriving today. Something about me now being a woman that there was something important for us to discuss."

"And more importantly, for you to *do*." The woman who spoke had seemingly appeared out of nowhere stood at the entrance of the barn with a stern look on her face. While the years had been kind to her, they hadn't stopped the frown marks on her face from remaining even when she was no longer frowning.

"Grandma," said Ember III finally breaking into a smile and running to give her a hug.

It was now Cinder who wore a concerned look on her face. "Mother," she greeted simply.

Ever serious, the elderly Ashlyn got right down to it. "I see you've become weaker over the years, my child. The wielder I trained would have never lost to a teenage girl."

Despite almost letting her die earlier, Ember III immediately stood up for her mother. "Well in her defense, Grandma, she did teach me everything she knows."

"Including how to use the Darkness to channel even more power?" Silence from both the younger Embers. "That's what I thought."

"Mother—" started Cinder who was immediately interrupted by her airways closing up with an almost effortless gesture from Ashlyn.

"You see," said Ashlyn, "how easy it is." She spoke the words as if instructing a lesson for both Cinder and Ember III. "Do you even remember this move, Cinder? Because at this stage of your daughter's training, I fully expect you to be holding nothing back. Am I clear?" Cinder didn't answer out of some misplaced sense of defiance which angered Ashlyn. "I said, am I clear?"

Cinder still didn't answer, far more concerned about her own daughter's *lack* of concern. "You know," said Cinder, barely able to breathe, "you sound just like father." These words immediately caused Ashlyn to let go and Cinder immediately started coughing.

Ashlyn had disappointment written all over her face. "Don't compare me to that weak little man." She then dusted herself off as if she'd actually been doing something physical. "Speaking of your father, it's time we had a very important discussion," she said before eyeing Ember III, "about your daughter's next step in her training.

A few minutes later, they were back inside the mansion, sitting at the dining room table, each with tea in front of them. Ember III knew well enough that she was here out of courtesy and wasn't a part of the conversation. And Cinder knew that her part was more of listener than speaker.

"So how is her training coming along, Cinder?"

"She's much further than I was at her age, mother."

Ashlyn put a hand up as if she didn't care too much for chit chat. "Yes, yes, but has she killed anyone yet?"

Both Cinder and Ember III shared a look. "She only just turned eighteen, mother. I don't think she'd need have a list of victims al—"

"Must I remind you that *you* were eighteen when you had your first kill?"

Ashlyn stiffened her jaw. But her twitch of anger wasn't because that kill was something she regretted at all, but rather because she didn't want to discuss this particular subject matter in front of her daughter. "I remember killing my father very well, yes. Thanks mother, for reminding me in front of my daughter."

"Well then perhaps I should also remind you, in front of your daughter, why it's so important that she begin killing people immediately. You know our cause: bringing Oswald back from the dead using synn power. And to do that we need the power of blood." She pointed at Ember III. "Her blood. She's a third generation darkwielder and we need to know if the power of a third generation is enough to get what we need or if we have to wait for *her* to have a child."

Cinder could not believe what she was hearing. It wasn't enough that she was making it blatantly obvious that she was simply using her grandchild for her own means but now she wanted to make a darkwielder out of her *great* grandchild? Did this woman's depravity know no bounds?

"First of all, mother, she's a third-generation *wielder*, not darkwielder. At least not yet. Second of all, you cannot seriously be considering passing on this curse to yet another generation, surely?"

Ashlyn didn't answer immediately and simply looked at her. "My child," she said as if something were obvious, "the only reason you were born was to bring back my brother. And that's the only reason she's here. As for any other reason for existing, it's for the freedom of wielders; to bring them out of service. And that's something you have not done for the fifty-three years you've been in this world." Ashlyn spoke the words as if an accusation before continuing. "And that's a transgression I can forgive because it was Oswald who had the mind to do just that."

"Mother, this is madness though. I mean, you don't truly expect to still be alive to see your great grandchild, do you?"

"There is a way, but it deals with very tricky power. But we'll get to that when Ember gives birth to a young one."

Cinder rolled her eyes. "Oh, good Light, mother."

"You know what, I think I should leave the room."

However, Ashlyn had other ideas. "Oh, I think you should stay. We have to talk about the next step in the plan."

"No. Ember, you can go. Me and mother have something to discuss in private." After Ember III politely left the room, Cinder turned all her attention to her mother. "Mother, this cycle truly has to stop."

Ashlyn looked at Cinder as if pitying her. "Oh my child, you don't really think that Ember should abandon the dark to be a wielder of *The Light* do you?"

"Of course not, mother. I know better than that. Whatever I am, I understand that being a darkwielder is the only thing that will give us the ability to free all the wielders and survive the fight that's sure to come. However, where I have a problem is with this idea that we do not have free will to choose for ourselves. That's my problem. I want my daughter to pick her own fate. If she picks *The Light*, then so be it. But if she picks the Darkness, then far be it for us to stand in the way."

311

For a moment, it looked like Ashlyn understood and simply raised her eyebrows in affirmation and swiftly moved on. "So, if this is how you feel, then I take it that preparations haven't been made for her upcoming kill; her first kill as it would be?"

"Well admittedly mother, arranging the death of a Lord is not exactly an easy thing to do. One cannot just do the deed and disappear."

"Indeed," said Ashlyn, her eyes turning cold, "which is why I thought it best that Ember's upcoming kill *not* be her father."

This both disturbed Cinder and got her curious. *If not Leonard, then whom?* "Who did you have in mind instead?" Cinder realized too late that she should have known the answer. When the Lange sword punctured through her chest having entered through her back, Cinder's blood had already been cold from the chill of the shocking reveal. She crumbled to the floor and died slowly, staying alive just long enough to hear Ashlyn and Ember's final conversation.

"How do you feel?" asked Ashlyn.

"I feel," said Ember III, "alive. Wow, this is so surreal."

"Good. Hold onto that feeling and allow it to fill you up every time you kill. Now, assuming your blood is not powerful enough, I'll need you to give birth to the fourth generation as soon as possible."

"And what will you do then, Grandma? Because mother was right. You could very well be dead by the time my child is of age."

"I have a plan for that. But if it is to work, it will require you *not* getting as attached to that child as your mother was to you. Because I am telling you now, by the time that child is your age, that child will no longer be the same."

Ember III nodded. "Understood." She then looked down at the still-dying Cinder. "I'm not as weak as she is," she said cold-heatedly.

*

313

By Bernard Bayede

THIRTY-EIGHT YEARS LATER

Somewhere in a thick forest, a fifty-six-year-old woman walked next to a seventeen-year-old girl. "Where are we going, mother?"

Ember IV was not the first person in her family to have the name Ember. In fact, her mother, grandmother and great grandmother had the name before her.

"Don't worry, Ember. Your great grandmother told us to meet here."

"Why? What's going on?" asked Ember IV.

"You'll know soon enough girl. Now hush." The woman who'd once called herself Ember but now went by the name Lavania, had never had any patience for her daughter. She'd distanced herself from her emotionally, just like her grandmother had told her to. And tonight, she was finally going to learn why. Unfortunately, her redhead daughter still had one last question left.

"Where are we?"

Annoyed, Lavania decided to answer this one last question in the hopes that getting an answer would shut her up for good. "We're in Hellepoint City. Now quiet."

To be specific, they were walking through the woods of Hellepoint Valley. If what she'd heard her grandmother tell her once was true, then just a mile ahead would be Lange Manor, where her and great grand Uncle Oswald grew up over a hundred years ago. But before they got to the manor, they came across a clearing in the woods where a woman stood in front of a fire.

The woman was much older than Lavania and Ember IV, perhaps even combined. In fact, her true age was well over a hundred but her looks betrayed that age as she barely looked a day out of her eighties. Lavania knew her secret. She knew that after the death of her daughter – Lavania's mother – the woman had found a unique way of using the black slumber crystal to suspend her aging. But the trade-off was that the suspension only worked in lengthy deep sleeps that

315

spanned years. As such, years went by without Lavania seeing her grandmother as she was hell-bent in seeing her great granddaughter become a woman. And now the time had come.

The original Ember smiled when she saw her great granddaughter. "Hello young one. You must be Ember."

It was Lavania who answered. "Ember, meet your great grandmother." No answer from the fourth generation.

"You have no idea how long I've waited to meet you." Ashlyn – as she'd called herself for a long part of her life – quickly moved on to business. "I trust your mother has taught you everything there is about being a wielder including how crystals work?"

Ember IV finally spoke. "Yes, she has. She's taught me everything about being a wielder and says I'm better than her, her mother and even you. In fact, the only thing she hasn't told me is what we're doing here in Hellepoint City."

"You're almost a woman now, Ember. In fact, I believe that your eighteenth birthday is in a few days and I thought it pertinent that you be brought here to complete your training."

"Mother told me about that too. This is about my first kill, is it not? My grandmother, your daughter, killed her father and my mother killed her mother. So, who is it that I am to kill?"

Ashlyn let out a breath. "Me." The oldest Ember let that sink in for both her kin. "The importance of your first kill cannot be understated. The point has always been not to kill under your own power but rather by allowing the Darkness to take over and give you the will. But in this case, killing me won't just imbue you with Darkness, but, due to you being the fourth generation, you will also receive the knowledge you need to revive Oswald."

Ember IV had heard all about her great grandmother's brother and how the past hundred years had been about bringing him back. But she had one important question she needed to ask. "Great Grandmother, if you're dead, how exactly are you going to reunite with Great Grand Uncle Oswald." Ember IV watched as Ashlyn answered by lifting a yellow crystal. "What's that supposed to do?"

Ashlyn snapped the crystal in two and put them in separate bowls before putting them over a fire. "Do you know what a yellow crystal does? It allows two wielders, each holding one half of the crystal, to communicate over long distances."

"Yes, I know what the yellow crystal does but what I don't know is what use it is to us right now." Ember IV suddenly felt a sharp object at her throat. It was her mother holding the famous indestructible sword at her throat. "Mother, what are you doing?"

"Fulfilling your destiny." She then nodded at Ashlyn.

"What's going on here?" asked Ember IV, confused.

It was Ashlyn who answered. "You asked what the yellow crystal is for? Well, as I'm sure you know, the crystals can do pretty amazing things far beyond the power that everyone else is aware of depending on what you add to it and the state of the crystal when you use it. Well," continued Ashlyn, "as it turns out, when you combine the yellow crystal melted into a liquid with the blood of a dying person, the person who drinks this potion – provided that the dying person drinks the melted crystal twin – will permanently have the dying person's consciousness in them for the rest of their life."

Ember IV couldn't believe what she was hearing so she had to confirm it, almost too shocked to speak the words. "Wait, are you saying that if I drink a melted yellow crystal with your blood in it, then you'll be in my head forever?"

Ashlyn nodded with a sinister smile on her face. "That's correct."

"And what if I refuse?"

Lavania instinctively grabbed onto her daughter, keeping the sword at her throat. "You won't have a choice."

"You misunderstand, mother. I meant in my mind. What if, after you've forcefully etched her consciousness into me, I refuse to allow it to take control of me? What if I force it to linger at the back of my mind for the rest of time as that irritating but ignorable voice in my head? What then?" Unfortunately, Ember IV saw that she'd spoken far too soon as she saw Ashlyn produce a small black crystal no bigger than a pearl. Ember IV knew immediately what the purpose of the slumber crystal was. "No. No, *no!* Mother, tell her to stop!"

"I'm sorry my child but this is your destiny. It's what you were born to do."

Ember IV thought of all the ways she'd been taught to get out of this. Unfortunately, all the training in the world was no use against two highly experienced darkwielders. In just a matter of minutes, they had exacted their plans and Ember IV could do nothing but watch as she was forced to swallow the black crystal that would silence her thoughts permanently and then be forced to drink the melted yellow crystal with Ashlyn's blood which she'd provided with effortless slits of the wrists. As Ember IV watched Ashlyn fall to the ground and die, she simultaneously felt her own mind die as it got taken over by her great grandmother.

Lavania had watched her daughter lose consciousness, understanding that that would be the last of her. She looked at her grandmother who took her final breath just as her daughter woke up, as the original Ember, now reborn. "Grandmother?"

Ember took a moment to admire her work and look at her new body. "Please, Lavania, call me Ember."

Lavania smiled. While she'd never readily admitted it to anyone, she was a big admirer of her grandmother and would have done anything to see the original Ember in the prime of her life. She'd heard stories about her and how she'd take on her enemies with a crystal in one hand and the white crystal-coated sword in the other. And now that she was back, it was time to give her what was hers.

Lavania presented the sword to her and watched the original Ember take it with a smile on her face. "What will you do Ember, now that you are whole again?"

"The time has come," said Ember. "The success of this ritual is proof that there is power in the blood of this generation and now I can feel it, coursing through my veins. You ask me what I will do? First I will find the source of all my pain and take out my revenge on her."

Lavania knew who she was talking about: the evil blonde vyren that killed Oswald. But Lavania was confused because this surely wasn't the plan she'd spent three lifetimes planning. "But what about the plan to bring your brother back?"

Ember smiled. "That *is* the plan, my darling Lavania." Ember saw the confusion on Lavania's face. "I told you that the bloodline was the answer to how to bring Oswald back. I told you that only someone with power in their blood could attain the knowledge to bring him back. And when I was between death," she said pointing her sword at her old body, "and life," she said pointing to her new body, "I was given the answer."

"What is the answer?"

"In order for Oswald to be revived, I must take a powerful body to the Nite Pole and sacrifice it directly to the Darkness. And then, in return, my brother will be born again."

Lavania felt like she missed something. "But what about the power of the synn? I thought the point of all this was to figure out how to use their power or something to that effect?"

Another smile from Ember. "It is. As it turns out, the venom coursing through each and every vyren in this dimension comes from the blood of the synn. We never needed to retrieve the power because the power lives in them. A power that, one day, the synn will return to take back. But until then, all we need is a vyren with venom that's a century old. And I just so happen to know the perfect vyren to fit that description."

Lavania was with her. "Theodora Lange."

*

PRESENT DAY
Year 817, ADI

Ember had loved the poetry of everything coming full circle with it beginning with Theodora and now ending with her. Unfortunately, all of that had almost been undone when she arrived at the dilapidated Lange Manor only to find two bladeslingers arriving presumably to arrest Theodora who was hiding in the dungeons. Ember had acted quickly.

When the two bladeslingers had surfaced with her prize, she'd fought them off, knocking one out and vaporizing the other with power Ember didn't even know she had. She then dropped Theodora into a slumber by tucking a black crystal down her top.

Ember had then used another red crystal to pull Theodora away as if towing her.

Ember had managed to make it all the way to the harbor where Lavania had been waiting. It had been a few weeks since the ritual. Ember had to admit that she was impressed with her granddaughter. She was far more obedient than Cinder and was far more worthy of the name Ember.

When she'd gone up to her, ready to say goodbye before she took off, she found Lavania with a worried look on her face. "Lavania darling, what's wrong?"

"While I was securing your transportation to Noctovia, I heard the strangest of rumors."

"Rumors?"

"I think a storm might be coming. Apparently the vyrens have a leader and all of them, at least in this city, answer to him."

This was the first that Ember was hearing of this and she'd lived over a hundred years. "And what of this?"

325

"She's going to be missed, grandma."

"Don't call me that. And why should I care about some vyren leader I've never heard of? Why should I care whether she," said Ember, kicking Theodora, "lives or dies?"

"I'm not saying whether you should or shouldn't, Ember. I'm just saying that by kidnapping her, you might be making enemies out of the undead who, by the way, have the means of creating an undead army of wights if you ever return to this city."

Ember had had enough and closed the gap between them. "Now you listen here, child. This place is my home, and I will not accept this idea that these undead beasts are going to dictate what I do. *When* I return, I'll be doing so with my brother and he won't be returning with just his darkwielder powers but with the power of synn meaning no vyren will be a match for him. Understood?"

Lavania hesitated before answering. "And what if I told you that they say that this vyren leader also has the power of the synn."

Ember was taken aback. "That's impossible. How," she said, barely able to even comprehend the weight of her own question, "how could a vyren gain access to synn power?"

"I don't have the answer, but I am quite certain it has something to do with a darkwielder helping him out."

This is interesting. This is very interesting. Had this darkwielder, who was seemingly working with this vyren leader, somehow gotten their hands on one of those synn statues and then somehow managed to acquire blood from it? If that was somehow possible, then why wasn't she doing that instead of dragging Theodora's body all the way across the world?

Because that power is diluted my sister.

Ember knew that voice. She'd started hearing it after slitting her wrists and bleeding out. She'd been afraid that the voice would leave her once she'd jumped into her great granddaughter's body but instead it had stayed with her. It was that voice that had spoken to her and given her the knowledge she'd been in search of for a hundred years. Fortunately, she was able to communicate with it without speaking.

What do you mean, Oswald?

Do you not see? This vyren king can only access part of the synn power. When I return, I will return as a synn. I will be all powerful, like the Darkness incarnate.

You will be a synn?

Yes. And when I return, I will be able free wielders from this slavery forever.

While Ember had never argued with her brother or doubted the plan, part of her wondered if this was what he wanted. His dying wish had been for her to stay away from the darkness. *Is this what you really want, brother? Do you really want to become a synn?*

328

After everything that you've done in my name, is there any other option than to go through with this? After all, this is the only way to get me back. Now go.

It was done. The time for questions was over. Oswald was right. Even if she was second-guessing herself now, she'd come too far for anything short of bringing her brother back. And no vyren, leader or not, was going to stop her, whether he had a darkwielder on his side or not.

"None of this matters, Lavania. I'm going to Noctovia and that's the end of it."

*

Ember wished that that had been the end of it. She really did. But it appeared that fate had different ideas for her journey. From the moment she left Hellepoint for the shores of the snow-ridden country of Noctovia, she was in an uphill battle. It began in truth when she realized that she was being followed in another ship. She knew that it had to be the bladeslinger that she allowed to live when she captured Theodora.

Fortunately, it appeared that the bladeslinger had stowed away on a pirate ship and when they saw a ship from Tandem Solaris, heading to Emperia, they'd changed heading, forgetting all about the ship Ember was on.

Eventually, the ship got as close as it dared to Noctovia and Ember used a boat to get to the icy land. She'd then started her journey for the Nite Pole and managed to make it all the way to a frozen lake where she found a polar bear that was missing an eye. Armed with her indestructible sword and a red crystal, Ember made quick work of the bear.

She'd planned to leave it for dead before getting an idea and excreted some of Theodora's venom and rubbed it into the bear's wounds just before it died. Ember wasn't even across the lake when the bear came back to life. But unlike Theodora, it wasn't a vyren but a wight meaning that it was a mindless entity that only had thirst for blood, period. Assuming that the bladeslinger somehow survived the ship battle that inevitably occurred between the pirate and Solari ships, then he'd also have to get through the bear.

Ember eventually found her way to an ice cave where she saw a beautiful Solari woman with a collection of twigs and branches in her hands. After exchanging pleasantries – with the woman introducing herself as Katalie – Ember asked the woman how to get to the Nite Pole at which point she dropped the branches and tried to run but to no avail as Ember grabbed her with her mind and pointed her sword at her.

It only got worse when a Bantu man came out of the cave, saw the scene of Ember holding her woman hostage and immediately tried to attack her. Ember was faster than him used a black crystal along with the red one to suspend him in mid-movement with her mind. Fueled by the Darkness egging her on, Ember then drove her sword through Katalie, killing her. However, she was taken aback when the Bantu man's bones began to crack.

It took Ember a minute to figure out what was going on, but being over a hundred years old, there was very little that Ember didn't know and understood this transformation to be that of a meta-morpher – known locally as meqa-moya. She knew that they were terrifying beasts and that a black crystal that small was no match for the magic coursing through the young man's beastly veins. Ember quickly moved on.

It wasn't long before she'd reached the summit of the mountain and finally laid eyes on the Nite Pole, shrouded in smoke and began her long descent down the mountain. As she got closer, the red-orange glow from the void that was the bottom of the mountain grew more intense. It was only when she got halfway that she realized that she was still being followed. While one of them looked like the bladeslinger that'd been following her before, there was another with him and she appeared to be a woman. But all of this was no matter as they wouldn't reach her by the time she was at the bottom.

Ember reached what looked like the top of a cliff face and finally came to a stop. Leaving Theodora at the start of the cliff, Ember made her way to the edge and dropped to her knees. It was finally time. After a hundred years, it was time to bring her brother back. Remembering the words that Oswald had taught her, she recited them.

"I stand here in the dark, kneeling to its majesty as its servant and I present tribute. Here I am, cast in shadows to ask for the power to conjure from death a fellow servant of the Darkness." At that moment, the red-orange glow grew stronger and Ember could feel its power. Unfortunately, she was no longer alone.

"Why hello there, Miss Wright," said the bladeslinger.

She recognized the bladeslinger and recalled his name. "Brother Jeff Longhunter. My, my, you are a persistent one."

As they began to banter, Ember never lost focus on her objective and made a point to channel the Darkness through her so that when they finally began fighting, she wasn't just relying on her sword fighting skill. While she had decades upon decades of experience with the weapon, relying on the Darkness always ensured success and this day was no different.

Ember finally managed to get the advantage over the bladeslinger and kicked him over the edge. She then heard his lady friend scream "no" and Ember turned to find this woman trying to move Theodora. Knowing that she could not let this happen, Ember advanced at the woman, intent on killing her. However, before she got to her, she felt a sharp pain hit her in the back.

Ember turned around to find the bladeslinger hanging off the edge of the cliff, still very much alive. Knowing that she couldn't very well kill the woman while the bladeslinger still lived, Ember pulled the knife out of her back and charged towards the bladeslinger. The fight was just as one-sided as it had been before but just when Ember had the bladeslinger kneeling and at the mercy of her sword, she heard a familiar voice.

"Ember!?"

Ember turned around and was shocked to see Theodora Lange, awoken from her slumber.

'Theodora."

"We need to talk."

Ember shook her head. "What is there to talk about?"

"How about the fact that that's my father's sword and I would like it back."

Ember looked at the sword – a weapon that had long since become an extension of her and her violence – and scoffed. "This sword? Do you know how many people I've killed with this thing?"

"I think I'll still be taking it back."

"If you want this back, then come and get it!" When Theodora did exactly that, Ember immediately parried but felt like she was fighting a ghost as Theodora moved with a speed that was incredible to comprehend. Eventually, Ember found herself being shoved backwards towards the void. However, she also managed to grab hold of Theodora and hung on for dear life.

Ember managed to move herself behind her enemy and stood over her. "Well Dora, here we are again with you at my mercy and your father's sword at your throat."

"You know that can't kill me," she spat.

"I don't want you dead. I want you sacrificed," said Ember as she slowly dragged Theodora to the edge. "You see, that's your destiny, Dora."

"That's not my destiny," said Theodora, struggling. "And my name is Theodora!"

Before Ember could tell her that she didn't care, she saw the bladeslinger, now covered in blood, standing back up despite looking like he'd been through Lloomis. And far behind him, up the mountain was another man wearing armor and armed with a sword running down the mountain. It was at this moment that Ember knew that the fight was lost.

The thought horrified her. *How could this have happened!?* After all the planning, literally a hundred of years leading to this one moment, how had it all come undone like this? But Ember didn't have time to dwell on the negative. She had to focus on getting out of here alive. That was the only way that she could hope to fight another day because there was definitely going to be another day.

Ember allowed the Darkness to fill her up and suddenly felt like letting out all her anger over this failure and looked to the Heavens and screamed. The scream was something so unholy and so monstrous that there was no way that it had come from her or anything else that wasn't the Darkness. As her scream drowned out all other noise, it was accompanied by a release of energy that shot out of the void.

The energy rose into the air before suddenly exploding outwards. Ember wasn't sure what happened next but what she did know was that somehow, the explosion had caused her to be sent flying through the air and clear over the mountain because she woke up on the frozen lake. While she didn't actually remember flying through the air or even landing on the lake, she knew that it was the Darkness that put her there because she was the only one who'd ended up on the lake.

Ember looked across the lake and saw the dead polar bear – now truly dead – and wondered if that wasn't a sign. A bear that had been alive, fought some kind of battle and survived only to be killed and then revived was now truly dead. Was this not a symbol of her plan? A hundred years and here she was, her plan, dead in the water.

Ember also wondered if this was the work of *The Light.* Oswald's last words had been for her not to give into the Darkness and she'd betrayed that all in an effort to see him again and now her plan had gone up in smoke. Was it perhaps because it wasn't meant to come true?

Unfortunately, none of this mattered as she got up and started the slow journey back to Emperia. If she was going to have to come to terms with her failure, then she was going to do it in Hellepoint, the place she called home. Only there was also a vyren leader who called the place home too. But that didn't matter. All that mattered was that she was alive which meant she'd find another opportunity. She only hoped that it wouldn't take another one hundred years.

By Bernard Bayede

THE LAST OF THE ARKERS

Twyler remembered the day that it had all come to an end for his kind: the day the arkers fell. It was a tragedy in the truest sense of the word because arkers were a peaceful people. They were obedient people and most importantly, they were faithful people. That was why *The Light* saw it fit to bless them with their own dimension called Fairden: a world of green hills and mountains that was the epitome of peace. When arkers were living on these lands in harmony, they were performing their sacred duty on behalf of *The Light*.

When *The Light* created arkers, it'd created them for one purpose: to answer the prayers of the mortals that it had made incarnate in its own image. 'Hear the prayer; interpret the prayer and answer the prayer', that was the mission. As such, the tales of arkers descending from the heavens to save the lives of mortals were endless… until that day.

Some said the arkers should have seen the attack coming. After all, not only did they have preternatural speed, strength, heightened senses and the ability to heal themselves and others, but they also had the clairvoyance to sense the prayers of others when they were in danger. So why couldn't they sense their own peril coming? Others said that the arkers couldn't have known the attack was coming because there was no way for beings from other dimensions to enter Fairden. The gateways from the other dimensions to Fairden didn't work unless one were an arker or, as it turned out, had the power of an arker.

The attack itself had been devastating as every arker in Fairden had been killed. While the story of eradication of the arkers travelled from dimension to dimension, becoming famous quite quickly, the story of who did it remained a mystery. Some said it was the bladeslingers of Emperia in the mortal dimension (who would go on to earn the nickname 'bloodslinger' due to the rumor) while others said it was darkwielders. No one truly knew who the culprits were. But that wasn't the only thing that no one knew. The other thing that people couldn't know was that there were still arkers alive!

Twyler Rench had been on a mission when Fairden was attacked. He'd been answering the prayer of a farmer from Tandem Solaris. He'd immediately known that something was wrong when he felt a pain deep inside himself. It was followed by an instinct that told him not to go home. It wasn't until the dust had settled that Twyler had attempted to return to Fairden only to realize that he couldn't and that he was stuck in the mortal dimension.

That had been 300 years ago. Ever since discovering that he was stuck in the mortal dimension, Twyler had been forced to adapt. It hadn't been easy but thanks to the residents of Tandem Solaris remembering all the good the arkers had done on their behalf, the Solari had done well by him, not only allowing him to stay but also being willing to give him anonymity from the rest of the world.

The fact and the matter was, it was no longer safe to be an arker in the mortal dimension. Bladeslingers, who once only hunted vyrens, now had no qualms hunting anything even remotely supernatural including the few arkers that were left forcing those still alive to hide in plain sight as mortals, never revealing their true selves lest news of their nature reach the Emperian government and the edgemen descended on them.

As such, Twyler had spent the past few centuries living a quiet life as a farmer. Due to the fact that he aged slowly – thanks to his healing abilities – he didn't look a day older than 43. In fact, if he used his arker powers as regularly as he used to, he'd have been aging even slower. Twyler had chosen the farmer's life because it reminded him the most of Fairden where arkers spent most of the time looking after the endless green fields and being one with nature.

Twyler enjoyed the serenity of farming. He enjoyed the solitude and the notion of using his hands to get things done. Back in the good days, he'd only get this feeling when he saved lives. But now, bailing hay; looking after animals and producing farm stock was his way of feeling whole. While Twyler didn't use his powers nearly as much as he used to, he still found use for them while working around the farm. It was the only way he could manage a whole farm by himself. Yet despite living out in the middle of nowhere, he still bumped into people from time to time.

While it was imperative that he interact with the people that he sold the farm stock to in exchange for gold crystals; he'd also found himself becoming something of a special counsel to the Solari chiefs during important moments. Then of course there were the nosey kids who just had to see the legendary arker with their own eyes that came sneaking onto the farm. Twyler always sensed them a mile away. But the only run-ins with people that Twyler paid any mind to were the close calls, like the time twenty years ago when he'd risked going down to the port to deliver his stock to a ship departing to Hellepoint and got spotted by a sailor. Of course, Twyler should have known better as a man like him with the dark skin of a Bantu stuck out like a sore thumb in a continent where people had lighter more russet skin with red cheeks and straight black hair.

Fortunately, the sailor that had spotted him hadn't been there by accident and had in fact been looking for him. York, as the sailor was known, had been sent by another arker that Twyler had thought dead. It was only in that moment when York had stood face to face with him to tell him that she was alive that Twyler remembered that he had not been the only one that had been on a mission when Fairden had been attacked.

While York would relay the message from the arker known as Camryn to come to Pscycopolis where she was hiding, Twyler would decline, claiming that he was where he was meant to be. Over the years, York would return with news from Camryn and Twyler would send him back with his own news. Eventually twenty years went past with York, every time, failing to get Twyler to budge. But as Twyler stood on his front porch today, looking up at the rings that surrounded the world and remembering his old home of Fairden, he could sense that today was going to be different.

The source of an arker's power was his faith in *The Light*. But after the devastation of Fairden, Twyler's faith was not what it used to be and that had affected his powers. He was not as fast as he used to be nor able to heal as fast as he used to. But the worst was his ability to sense when mortals needed his help. Even now, while he could sense that it was York making his way on horseback, down the gravel road, he couldn't tell if everything was alright.

Twyler hadn't moved from where he was standing as York dismounted his horse and approached him. "Did you know that this dimension was the first created by *The Light* after the Heavens?" Twyler had pointed to the brightest of the rings in the sky.

York was used to Twyler's philosophical statements. He didn't bat an eye and instead went to stand with Twyler on the porch. "I thought it would have created Fairden first."

"Oh no, Fairden came much later as a reward to the arkers after the war."

"The war against the synn?" This, York knew all about as he'd had many questions when he was younger about being a warrior. It had taken him years to mature into someone who didn't glorify war.

Twyler nodded. "Yes. While the Underworld always existed as a place where evil was sentenced to, this dimension, the mortal dimension, was the first dimension created by *The Light*. You see, *The Light* wanted to create beings of flesh and life to see if they would worship it out of their own free will. While it had already created the arkers, arkers were created to serve a purpose, a function: to stomp out evil. Mortals were created out of love."

"So then how did the other dimensions come to be?"

"Well, the Darkness, not to be outdone, created the synn, as you know, to spread evil and they wanted to spread it to the mortal dimension, but *The Light* wasn't having any of that. At first, *The Light* told the Darkness to create its own dimension and do with it as it saw fit and that's how the Ashlands dimension came to be." Twyler pointed at the bright red ring, neatly wedged between the white one and a brown one. "But of course, the Darkness wasn't satisfied with what it had created and wanted the mortal dimension, so *The Light* and the Darkness proposed a war for the soul of this dimension." Twyler pointed to the brown ring.

"Lloomis," said York, knowing all about the battlefield of the war.

"Yes. The Lloomis dimension was created for the sole purpose of the war between the arkers and the synn. Of course, you know how that ended."

York did. "The synn were soundly defeated and turned into stone for their trouble."

"That was done to prevent anyone from trying to access their power from their carcasses," he said before Twyler's mind wandered somewhere else. "If only we'd done the same thing with the daminites then we wouldn't have those damn tandemites that those cursors are so fond of."

"I'm not sure that would have worked," said York. "Those statues perched on the tall buildings in Pscycopolis; some believe that vyrens acquired their powers by figuring out how to drain synn blood from them."

Twyler laughed softly. "Vyrens are the work of darkwielders, York. Nothing more. Darkwielders with terrible imaginations. Speaking of imagination, we arkers always joked that *The Light* didn't really have any imagination when it created the different dimensions since they all have the same geography. The Lite Pole and the Nite Pole are located in the same place and Emperia, Kingdom of Daun, the Bantulands and Tandem Solaris all exist there."

"I figured out that much when you mentioned the war taking place near the Nite Pole but on Lloomis." York screwed his brow. "What I can't figure is how the Limbo dimension came to exist."

"Ah," said Twyler sighing. "Limbo, limbo, limbo. Limbo is the only dimension not created by the Light nor the Darkness. It was created by darkwielders as a means to circumventing death. As you know, when any being dies, it either goes to the Heavens or the Underworld. Darkwielders knew this. So, in order to cheat death, the first thing they had to do was prevent the being from going to either place. To do this, they created the Limbo dimension. It was only after this that they would figure out the means of bringing them back. And that's how we got phantoms and wights and--"

"Vyrens," said York, following.

"Now you see why I say that their creation came from darkwielders." Twyler looked at the six colored rings that circled the world. "They say that all those dimensions surround this one with the Heavens above, the Underworld below and the others all around us and that's why the dimensions look like rings surrounding the world from here." Twyler smiled at the notion. "Now, I'm sure you didn't come all this way out here to listen to an old man go on and on," said Twyler finally turning around to see York in a white Dress Uniform, decorated with honors that he'd earned since the last time Twyler saw him.

"Oh I don't know," said York. "As an old man myself, I think I can relate to the idea of going on and on."

Twyler looked at York as if seeing him for the first time. Gone was the young man who seemed carefree with his dark hair that was a little too wild for a man in His Majesty's Navy. In his place stood a man with short-cropped hair that hid the greying temples and creases on his weathered forehead. Twyler saw that he was holding a hat in his hands and recognized the insignia. "*Captain* York, I see."

"It has been a while, hasn't it? You've never even seen my ship and I've commanded it for a decade already."

Twyler noticed the troubled look on the Captain's face. "Judging from the look on your face, it would not appear that you came here to celebrate your achievements."

York shook his head. "I'm here about Camryn, Twyler. She's been taken."

This news shocked Twyler but York wouldn't have had any way of knowing since the emotion didn't register on Twyler's face. "Taken?" he simply repeated.

York nodded. "The last time I went to see her, I found her place ransacked and no sign of her at all."

Still, Twyler did not emote a thing. "Was it the bladeslingers? Did they finally track her down?"

"I couldn't be sure about that, Twyler but I doubt it. While bladeslingers wouldn't make it known at all if they had caught an arker, as an officer of His Majesty's Navy, I'd reached out and I haven't heard a thing about bladeslingers doing anything in Pscycopolis."

"It still could have been them." *Darn it*, thought Twyler. *I warned you to be careful, Camryn. This was the reason I didn't want to come to Emperia. They're just too many of those blade-wielding hunters*. Of course, Twyler remembered that that wasn't the only reason he didn't want to leave Tandem Solari. York snapped him back to the present.

"I don't think so."

"Why not?"

"Because of the last thing she told me to tell you. I was on my way to telling you when I got the urge to go see her first. I'm guessing that was her arker way of trying to let me know she was in danger. Anyway, she wanted me to tell you that she'd found one of the paintings. Do you know what she was talking about?"

Shock overcame Twyler again. While he still didn't wear his emotion on his face, this time he had to sit down. "She's talking about the paintings of Eddison Randalf Kessler."

"Eddison Kessler, the explorer?" said York, baffled.

Twyler corrected him. "No. The exploring he only did to cover up his real mission: getting rid of Emperia's stockpile of crystals."

York nodded as he knew this already but was still confused. "I remember that from the academy. We learnt all about the Great Voyage of 492. What I don't remember is anyone telling me that he was a painter."

"He wasn't one by profession. The only reason he painted anything was because of what he was painting." Twyler looked at York, dead in the eye. "It was the future." Twyler watched as this set in for York. "In truth, Kessler was an inventor and pioneer in how the world could advance by innovating how they used crystals."

"You mean specifically how we use wielders and how they use the crystals." York had never liked the taste of how the Emperian government used wielders by putting them into service.

"Exactly. It's because of people like him that we have wielder-driven ferry boats; wielder-driven elevators, the way we communicate, and the list goes on."

York scoffed. "You say 'we' but if we're being honest, it's only Emperians that do that. It's so disgusting."

"Well, Eddison Randalf Kessler shared that disgust, believe me. But only after he saw something that made him change."

York was putting two and two together. "The future. He saw the future."

"Exactly. To this day, no one knows how he did it or even what he did to see it but when he did, he decided there and then to change his ways. There's a legend that he wrote the King a letter that explained why he wasn't bothering to explain what he saw and instead absconded with the cache of crystals."

"Okay, so what happened with the paintings?"

"That's the issue. He hid them away in different locations. Some say, all over the world during his voyage. Others say he hid them all in Emperia before he left for the voyage. Others say they never left Pscycopolis which is where he was from."

"And you think Camryn found them?"

"So she claims."

"And why was she looking for them?"

Twyler wanted to laugh at the old joke. "Because she thinks that they're prophecies." When Twyler saw York just looking at him, he knew he had to explain. "When we first learned about these paintings back in Fairden, we first thought they were a joke or a lie. Then, when Kessler left Emperia in such dramatic fashion causing an outpour of frustration from the people, we started to wonder if there was more to it. That's when one of the High Arkers suggested that Kessler's paintings were in fact prophecies."

"High Arkers?"

"Yes. High Arkers were the oldest arkers in existence and the ones arkers went to when they wanted clarity on some of the prayers from the mortals. As you can imagine, arkers could not answer each and every prayer as some of them weren't meant to be answered. Some suffering is meant to be, which means we couldn't interfere and that's why we needed the High Arkers to interpret them.

"Now here's where it gets interesting and why, I believe, Camryn was after the paintings. Only High Arkers are capable of making a prophecy. They also happen to be the only ones capable of knowing how to get in and out of Fairden unassisted."

A light bulb went off in York's head. "So that's what she wants. She wants to get back to Fairden?"

Twyler's face finally showed an emotion: longing. "We all do, Captain. We all do."

"But her way of doing it is what: see the paintings and somehow ascend into a High Arker and open the gate?" Twyler didn't respond. What would he say? "Okay, so then how does that lead to her being taken? Even if someone was after the paintings, which I think is safe to say are very rare, why take her?"

"Well, it's possible that whoever took her wanted exactly the same thing she wanted: to get to Fairden."

York's eyes widened. "Then we have to stop them. Surely they'll kill her after they figure it out then they'll have free passage to Fairden. We need to go rescue her."

Twyler contemplated York's idea. There was that part of him, buried deep inside that was benevolent and wanted nothing more than to follow York to Emperia, to Pscycopolis and rescue Camryn. But he couldn't. "I'm sorry York."

"What do you mean you're sorry?" York was angry now. "Are you honestly telling me that you'd rather stay here and farm than rescue one of your own? What, is it because you're scared?"

Twyler shook his head. "It's not because I'm scared, York."

"Then what is it?"

Twyler was still reluctant, after all these years, to speak the words. But he did manage to find words he was willing to speak. "Did Camryn ever tell you how she ended up in Pscycopolis?"

"What?" York was dumbfounded by the sudden change in topic.

"When Fairden fell, did she ever tell you why she was in Pscycopolis?" Twyler didn't wait for him to answer. "That's where her last mission had taken her. Someone had prayed, asking for help from up above and they'd said that there were lives at stake and they needed *The Light* to come and save them. So, Camryn was sent down.

"As it turns out, the danger that had been posed was from vyrens. While I'm still not sure what in lloomis they were up to, they were killing people, sacrificing them and Camryn put a stop to it. When Fairden fell, she decided to remain there, scared that if she left and with no other arkers left alive, Pscyopolis would be there for the vyrens' taking."

"What does that have to do with…?" York trailed off when he realized what Twyler was getting to. "Wait, are you trying to tell me that you're still here because you're still completing your last mission?" Twyler's silence spoke volumes to York. "And what's your mission?" Twyler remained silent again which, this time, frustrated York. "Well, can you honestly say that hanging onto a mission three hundred years later is worth more than saving Camryn's life?"

"Our mission comes first, York. Not our lives. Our lives are lived in servitude of the Light. Camryn knows that."

York had heard enough and had already started walking. He only came to a stop to say one last thing. "I'm going to save her with or without your help. But I hope you change your mind."

*

It had been hours since Captain York had left. His request had given Twyler a lot to think about, but he also believed that he'd made the right decision. That still didn't keep his mind from being busy. Fortunately, there was one trusty way that Twyler knew to quieten it. Twyler made his way into the barn, took off his shirt and sat on the ground, legs folded, and eyes closed. He was going to meditate on *The Light*.

As Twyler breathed in and out, he allowed *The Light* to flow through him. Twyler wasn't a very bulky man but he was well defined. But that wasn't what stood out on his body. That was his arker tattoos which went all the way up his arms and then down his back. Black against his chocolate brown skin, the markings didn't stand out much. But when Twyler felt *The Light*

361

radiate through him, the tattoos came to life, glowing yellow and moving around.

"Light above, hear me and guide me down my path," prayed Twyler. As his tattoos glowed brighter and brighter, Twyler began to feel his mind quieten and then drift into his past… into his mission. He saw his failure. In his mind, he saw Lady Lakewalker perish at the hands of a metamorpher and how the metamorpher was devastated by the loss. His mind then moved on to the separation of the tribe into five smaller ones… all because he'd failed his mission.

Still connected to the past through his meditation, Twyler felt something bother him. He smelt it to. It smelt like fire. Now in tune with the danger that *The Light* was warning him about, Twyler opened his mind to his senses and then it hit him. He knew what the danger was. Twyler's eyes shot open and in a magnificent blur of golden light and soft sparks, Twyler took off running in unthinkable speed.

Within seconds, Twyler had run across his farm, the neighboring farm miles away and into the next farm where a fire raged on inside the wooden barn. As soon as Twyler was inside, he heard someone screaming from above.

"Somebody help me!" screamed a girl no older than fourteen.

"Hold on S'kay, I'm coming." Twyler was upstairs in a blur. However, before he could come back down, he noticed someone downstairs.

"Wow. The paintings were true. As I live and breathe: an arker, here in the flesh." The man who spoke was tall and skinny.

With the fire still raging on, Twyler was in no mood to talk but with this person in his way, what choice did he have? "Who are you and what are you doing here?"

"Oh, my apologies," said the man. "My name is merely Landon, but it is who I speak for that matters more. I speak for Lady Lilyn."

"Who is Lady Lilyn?"

The man looked confused by the question. "Why she's one of the archvyrens," said the man. Twyler's face gave away nothing leading the man to believe he hadn't really explained anything. "A General in the Vyren King's army?"

There's a Vyren King now? But Twyler didn't have time for this. "So, you're a vyren. That's good to know. But if you don't mind, I'm going to take this little girl to safety," he said, picking S'kay up and going back downstairs. Unfortunately, Landon remained in the way.

"I'm afraid I can't let you do that. I was ordered to kill you and—" That was it from Landon as Twyler kicked him with all his arker strength, sending him flying out of the barn. Twyler then walked outside and put S'kay down.

"Are you okay? Are you hurt?"

S'kay just looked at him with her big brown eyes. "You're the arker." Twyler simply nodded. "Why did you save me?"

"Because you asked me to."

"No, but I mean. I'm nobody. Nobody would miss me if I was dead except my aunt and uncle. You could have been saving more important people but you--"

"You are important S'kay." Twyler then heard something from across the farm. "But I'll have to tell you why later. Right now, I have to destroy this thing. So what I want you to do is run inside to your Aunt and—" Twyler had barely finished the sentence when Landon, using vyren speed, came rushing at him in a blur and sent him flying through the air.

Landon had hit him so hard and so fast that Twyler had landed back in his own barn. He was barely to his feet when Landon began to pummel him. Not to be outdone, Twyler turned the tables and began punching him back. They eventually made it back to their feet and fought so hard and fast that within a minute, the barn was no more.

Twyler eventually got Landon down and at his mercy when Landon began laughing. "What's your plan now? Surely you know a vyren can only be killed with human bone to the heart."

"And who told you that?" Twyler then placed a hand on the vyren's head and channeled *The Light* making his tattoos glow. The brighter they glowed the more Landon screamed. "You see, there are other ways to vanquish evil. My preferred way: damnation. A one-way trip to the Underworld."

"What!?" screamed Landon, now realizing his predicament. "No, no, please! Don't kill me."

"Technically, this wouldn't be considered killing. Arkers can't kill. But that wasn't my intention anyway. I need answers first starting with whether you were after the girl?"

"What!?"

"S'kay! Were you after S'kay?"

"No. We were after you! We know nothing about the girl."

"Then why burn her barn down with her inside it?"

"Because we knew that you would come."

"How?" Landon didn't answer and Twyler began to glow again. "How?"

"The painting!" said Landon, desperately. "The painting depicted it. We saw you rushing to the rescue when her barn caught fire with her inside!"

It was in this moment that Twyler realized how real this was. The paintings really did depict the future. They even went as far as to depict how Twyler would react if S'kay's life were in danger. This was unbelievable. Unfortunately, he'd revealed his hand to the vyren.

"Who is she anyway?"

That was enough for Twyler, who, still with his hand on Landon's forehead, began to glow brightly as Landon screamed until he screamed no more, and his body crumbled to dust. It had been a while since Twyler had vanquished an evil being. It was times like this that he remembered that an arker's original

367

function was to be a *soldier* of *The Light*. But there were more important things on Twyler's mind.

It dawned on him that staying in Tandem Solaris just to complete his mission might actually put his mission in danger. Now that these vyrens had the paintings, him staying here actually put his mission in jeopardy. So now he had to leave. He had no choice. He had to go to Pscyopolis and save Camryn and recover those paintings.

After checking that S'kay had made it home, Twyler did not waste any time. Twyler blurred into the house, picked up whatever he thought essential for the trip – which mostly came down to the clothes on his back – and blurred all the way across Tandem Solaris and back to the docks where he first met York. It was time to leave Tandem Solaris.

*

Sandara Windsalt had never been a jealous person, but currently, she couldn't help but feel small. Which was neither easy nor a good thing for a wielder from

Tandem Solaris. Unlike in Emperia where wielders were basically forced into the service of the government, and KwaBantu kaNoctovia where they lived in a kind of isolation from the tribes, Solari wielders had to prove their worth if they wanted to move up in the world. And there was no position more coveted by Solari wielders than that of 'first wielder': the right hand to the chief.

Sandara had decided to make her bones out at sea working for a respected sailor named Captain Jon York. It was not by accident that she'd decided to work for a foreigner with the idea being that if she could prove herself in so-called hostile territory, then it would mean more in the long run. It was her job to defend the ship from supernatural elements like pirate ships crewed by vyrens and storms conjured by darkwielders. That was her job.

So when an arker – the first that Sandara had ever seen in the flesh – blurred onto the ship and was welcomed with open arms by York, Sandara couldn't help but feel a little uneasy. How could she prove that she was the powerhouse of the ship if there was an almighty arker on the vessel?

They were a day into their journey when York noticed her discomfort. "Something on your mind Sandy?"

"Nothing you need to worry about, Captain?"

"On the contrary, everything that happens on this ship is for me to worry about. Is this about our guest downstairs?"

Sandara knew that there was no hiding anything from York now. "Why do we need an arker on this mission Captain? Do you not believe me powerful enough to handle whatever's ahead?"

"It has nothing to do with that."

"Then what does it have to do with then?"

"We're on our way to rescue an arker. It only makes sense that we have an arker come along with us."

"Hmm. So, it has nothing to do with the fact that we're going to a city that's infested with vyrens and you need the savior to save our asses?"

York gave Sandara a long look. "Sandy, I don't doubt your abilities. I know you can take on anything in your way. And over and above that, I also know that one day, you will be the first wielder of your tribe."

Sandara didn't answer immediately, instead taking the words in. "Well thank you for the vote of confidence, Captain but I never had any doubt I was going to become first wielder." Sandara then walked away, making her way to the front of the ship. Sandara had always had a tough exterior but it was a necessary evil in her line of work. Considering what she faced on a regular basis, it was the only way to ensure success.

While Sandara had intended to be alone at the front of the ship, intent on watching the sun set by herself, she saw that the front was already occupied by her least favorite person: the arker, Twyler Rench.

"I feel I should apologize. I understand that this is where you go at this time of day."

"Oh yeah. Is this your clairvoyance at work? If you knew I'd be here, then why are you here?"

"I also understood that you needed to get something off your chest as far I'm concerned. And my powers don't work that way."

"How do they work?

"They're based on faith. The more we believe in *The Light*, the more powerful we are. So you see, we arkers aren't all-powerful. So you don't need to feel threatened by--"

"Whoa, whoa, whoa. I don't recall saying that I was threatened by you or your powers. My concern has nothing to do with any animosity I have towards you. I'm sure you're a good guy."

"Wouldn't be much of an arker if I wasn't," joked Twyler.

"But I have a destiny that requires me to take on the toughest supernatural threats out there. And you being here is doing me no favors, alright."

Twyler gave her a smile and nodded. "Well rest assured that I have a destiny too and it doesn't have anything to do with me being out here on this vessel." Twyler sighed. "My destiny is back in Tandem Solaris."

This was interesting to hear. "What is it, your home or something?"

Twyler nodded. "Has been for the past three centuries."

"Huh. Well, I know you're originally from the Fairden dimension, but I've always been curious. Your complexion would suggest that you're from Noctavia-_"

"Actually, they prefer to call it the Bantulands—" quipped Twyler.

"But that's not true, is it? I mean, do the continents work the same way over there?"

"The continents are the same but the division between the people is non-existent. There are no races in Fairden. My complexion was chosen by me which I chose out of convenience since I frequented missions in the Bantulands."

"And you couldn't change it thereafter?"

"Why would I? Doing that would surely defeat the point of diminishing bias between races, would it not?"

"I'd never thought about that."

"Well that's why arkers exist. It's our job to educate you in the ways of *The Light* and help spread peace. Which is why what happened to us is so terrible. It's also why I have to go and save Camryn. This world cannot take one less arker soul."

Sandara felt like she was finally beginning to understand the arker except that she recalled something he'd said just a moment ago. "So, if Tandem Solari is not your home, then why do you say it's your destiny?"

Twyler didn't answer immediately and took a deep breath before answering. "There's someone back in Tandem Solari that I'm meant to protect. Someone who's very important to the future of the nation."

"Who are you talking about?"

"I can't say. The only way to protect her is to make sure that she goes about her young life completely unknown to the world or even herself."

"Wow. She's that important?"

"You have no idea." At that moment, something in Twyler stirred and he knew that there was danger coming. "Sandara, we need to get everyone down below. Something's coming."

"Is this your clairvoyance again?" said Sandara sarcastically.

"Yes. Yes, it is. Now please, do as I say."

Sandara was now on high alert, realizing that the arker was being serious. "What is it that's coming?"

"Vyrens."

Sandara did not need to be told twice. She immediately ran back to the Captain. The workers on the ship knew something was up when they saw the wielder of the ship running. "Captain, we're about to have company," said Sandara upon reaching the helm.

"What is it?" said York.

"The arker says its vyrens."

The Captain didn't need to be told twice either. "Men," he said loudly to the sailors on deck. "We are on the verge of being boarded. You're in for a fight so arm yourselves. I want every man on this ship holding an iron dagger before that sun sets," he said pointing to the setting sun on the horizon. He then turned to one of the younger crewmen. "Cabin boy, fetch my sword."

Sandara always smiled when the Captain asked for his sword. Part of the reason was because York's sword was one of the rare swords that was coated in white crystal making it indestructible. Allegedly, it had been passed on to him by his mentor and former

Captain of the ship. The other reason Sandara loved when York said that was because it meant she was about to get an opportunity to prove herself. "Captain, my orders?"

York pointed at Twyler who was still standing at the front of the ship. "I want you and the arker working together when they attack."

"You want me working with him? But Captain, you know I work better alone."

"I know that. But together, you'll be a force to be reckoned with. And remember, this isn't about killing monsters, it's about saving sailor lives. Now go, that's an order."

Sandara knew better than to argue and went back to the arker. She'd been involved in enough sea battles to know what the Captain expected of her. She pulled a large red crystal and a large black crystal out of her pouch and prepared herself mentally for what she was about to do. "Okay, so the Captain says that he wants us working together on this."

377

"And what exactly would this be?"

"It's a battle which means we kill as many enemies as we can."

"Hmm. I'm sure the Captain is aware of my nature and knows that bloodshed is not possible for an arker. I am on this world to save lives, not take them. My priority in this battle will be to save as many sailors lives as possible."

"Yes, and we do that by killing those things. Have you ever fought an undead pirate?" Sandara knew that Twyler wasn't going to answer. "For starters, they're not all vyrens. Only the Captain is a vyren. His crew is composed of wights: undead humans who didn't complete the transition. Unlike vyrens, wights are mindless and only care about feeding on blood. And, unlike vyrens, wights can be killed with iron."

Twyler decided not to let Sandara know that he already knew all of that. "My point still stands; I don't kill any beings alive or dead. I can only deport them to the Underworld and that I can only do one at a time.

So, perhaps a better strategy for you and me would be to protect the ship from being boarded and allow our sailors to board their ship."

Sandara wanted to be furious but realized that this might actually be a sound strategy. "How would you do that?"

"Easily enough." He lay a hand on her shoulder. "While an arker cannot use a crystal's power, they can allow that crystal's power to last longer and they can increase the power of a crystal simply by laying hands on the wielder. So, what I'm proposing is that we stand right here and use that red crystal to freeze each and every wight on that ship in place while our sailors board the ship and cut them down with ease."

Sandara had to admit it was a good strategy but what was really selling her on this was the feeling of the crystals power growing in her hands as the arker spoke. She closed her eyes and allowed the power to radiate through her. When she opened them again, the vyren ship was upon them. "Time to see if this will work."

Sandara outstretched her hands and used her mind to slow the ship down just as it got to them. She then watched as the wights onboard tried to move only to find themselves frozen in place. The sailors, already used to supernatural things happening around them when Sandara was on board, did not hesitate and started climbing on board the other ship and the fight commenced.

The sailors were halfway through slaughtering their way to victory when Sandara noticed someone on the other ship. While it was clear that he was neither a vyren nor a wight, what made him stand out was his coat and hat. "Bladeslinger," said Sandara who immediately cut off her crystal attack and charged for the other ship.

"No wait, Sandara no!" But it was too late as Twyler's warning fell on deaf ears. What happened next was horrifying as the sailors were caught off guard by the sudden movement of the wights. While a few fell immediately, the rest adapted quickly and began fighting back. But it was clear that the advantage was gone. Unable to simply stand by and watch the men be slaughtered, Twyler gathered what power he could from *The Light* and immediately disappeared into a blur as he sped between both ships, pulling sailors out of danger and knocking what wights he could into the water.

As Twyler moved, he noticed Sandara still heading straight for the bladeslinger and decided to intervene. He moved between the two, grabbing Sandara and knocking the bladeslinger into the water. He then blurred them straight up to the Captain at the helm. "Captain, I think it's time to go. Their numbers have dwindled. They won't be pursuing."

Sandara watched as York nodded. "Wait what!? There was a bladeslinger on that ship and we're just going to leave him be!?"

"We're not here to kill bladeslingers, Sandy," said York. "This is a rescue mission, and we need to get going with it." York then spoke loudly to all the men. "Gentlemen, back to your stations with haste, now!"

As Sandara continued to fume knowing she could do nothing to finish what she started, she stared daggers through the arker. She only pulled away when she noticed someone on the other ship just as they sailed away from it. It was the vyren Captain and he didn't look nearly as displeased as Sandara imagined he would. Sandara wondered what that was about. When she looked back at the arker, he was also looking at the vyren Captain, except the arker looked like something had dawned on him. "What in the world is going on here?"

*

When Camryn woke up, she instinctively tried to move and immediately felt pain. Remembering her predicament, she immediately knew not to move. She opened her eyes to see a man dressed in black smiling at him. Except he wasn't a man at all but a vyren.

"Good morning sweetheart. Sleep alright?"

He knew the answer to that considering that he was the one who knocked her unconscious. Camryn was currently hanging from chains attached to the ceiling of the damp and dreary dungeon, with her feet just dangling off the ground. But that wasn't why she was in pain. Currently, there was a human bone dagger in her heart. Since bone daggers killed vyrens and not arkers, the bone sticking out of her was meant to be poetic. It was also preventing her from using her arker powers to heal.

"I'm not your sweetheart, bloodsucker."

"Ouch, so harsh. You know what," said the vyren, "just for that…" He then put his hand on the dagger handle and twisted it, making Camryn scream in pain.

"Is that completely necessary?" said another man walking into the room. This man was also a vyren but much more intimidating and taller than the first man. "We need her alive, after all."

"Don't lecture me, Oltore. You don't get to tell me what I do with my prize. Or have you forgotten that *I* am the one that captured her; that captured an arker?" There was a reason for him to be proud of the accomplishment and that was because it *was* an accomplishment, especially in this day and age where arkers were one in a thousand at most.

"How can I forget, Deux when you're always boasting about it?"

While Camryn was in perpetual pain, she didn't forget her training for missions even after all these centuries. Sometimes the best way to get out of situations wasn't by blurring through it but rather by having all the information. After all, arkers were tools of *The Light*, not blunt instruments. So, when they answered prayers, they needed to see the whole picture before they acted, lest they end up helping the wrong kind of person. So now, it was time to piece together the information.

"So, you're the one they call 'The Dreaded'?"

Both Deux and Oltore gave her a look. Oltore was amused while Deux was insulted. "I'll have you know that all archvyrens are called 'the dreaded'. I am known as Deux the Dreaded. Lilyn is known as Lilyn the Dreaded."

"Lilyn," said Camryn. "She's the seductrix, am I right? But even she hasn't earned the reputation like you have," said Camryn, gesturing to Oltore. "Where Lilyn is the seductrix, you're the intimidating one." Camryn then looked at Deux. "You," said Camryn, "I know nothing of you."

"Is that so? Well do you want to know what I think?" Deux answered by grabbing the dagger and twisting it again. Camryn screamed. "That's what I think."

Oltore laughed something of a growly chuckle. "You're going to torture her because she spoke the truth?"

"You call that a truth? Here's the truth, Oltore. In a matter of days, the arkers will be no more and the

Vyren King will finally be able to take his plan to the next stage."

"Hmm," said Oltore, not impressed. "You say this right in front of your prisoner? You give archvyrens a bad name."

"What's the concern? She'll be dead soon."

"Not according to the paintings. She must live long enough for us to capture the other arker. Or have you forgotten?"

"I haven't forgotten a thing, Oltore," said Deux quickly. "But what's the point of waiting? The trap has been set and if those paintings that we have are true, then that means the arker and his friends are already on their way."

"Yes, but that's assuming…"

"…you have the whole picture," said Camryn, still wincing from the pain.

Deux resisted torturing her again. "How would you know that we don't?"

"Because you don't know how many paintings there are. No one does. When you caught up to me, you found one in my possession. But one out of how *many*, you don't know."

"It doesn't matter," said Deux. "Because how many paintings we have won't derail our plans."

"You mean the King's plans, right?" Camryn noticed the look from both Deux and Oltore. It was a hard look, like they didn't like the fact that what Camryn spoke was the truth. Camryn decided to push this issue. "You two don't like the King, do you?"

"What business is that of yours whether we like him or not?"

Oltore proved that he was the smart one of the two when he said, "Deux, don't engage her on things we want her to know not of."

"Oh don't you talk down to me as well, Oltore," spat Deux. "You're not him. You don't command me."

"I get the feeling you hate being commanded," said Camryn. She took the fact that Deux didn't

387

immediately torture her as a sign she was onto the truth. "If you no longer believe in the cause of your master then why not leave his services?"

While Oltore tried to stop him from speaking, Deux persisted, clearly having wanted to get this off his chest for a while. "It's because of his power. The Vyren King isn't just the first vyren, he's the most powerful."

"Because of his age?" guessed Camryn.

"No, because his blood is undiluted." When Deux saw that Camryn didn't know as much about vyren mythology as he thought, he explained. "Unlike every other vyren in the world, the King wasn't turned. He didn't have to die with venom in his system. He was created with the blood of a synn."

Camryn's eyes widened. "That's impossible. All the synn were destroyed during the war. Worse actually, because they were turned into stone specifically so no one could try and access their power. I was there."

"Then you would know that that's not strictly speaking true. Not all of the synn were destroyed. One was left alive, remember? Sentenced to the mortal dimension, this dimension, to live out the rest of his life as a mortal with no power."

Camryn remembered this story. That synn was one of the Darkness' top generals. The punishment was meant to be a sentence worse than death because along with his powers, he would also lose his immortality, grow old and die. But that was 400 years ago. There was no reason to believe he was still alive… unless of course he'd found a way to become an immortal vyren!

"The Vyren King is the Synn General?"

Deux actually smiled. "Close. He's the son of the Synn General. The King's father knew that there was no way of reactivating his power. What, with his powers being stripped of him and his fellow synn being turned to stone and then placed in Pscycopolis to insult him, he resigned himself to finding a loophole. And find a loophole he did. He realized that while his son would be born mortal, he would be immune from being unable to use his blood for power and thus he turned his son into the first immortal vyren. You see, there's always been power in blood. And with every passing generation, that power grows."

Camryn couldn't believe it. "That's impossible. The power of a synn can't be transferred to a mortal. It would kill them."

"Not if they had the help of a darkwielder."

Camryn couldn't believe it. Foolish. That's what her and her fellow arkers had been when they allowed that Synn General to live. Now look at them. But Camryn didn't have the time or patience to think about a past long since passed. She refocused. "That's not why you hate your King though, is it?"

Deux sighed, as if the answer was obvious. "We hate the King because instead of taking over the human world with blood, fire and destruction, he's taking it by playing politics with that pathetic human King named Kandy."

"King Kandy?"

Oltore saw that Deux was about to continue explaining. "Deux, you need to stop t--"

Deux shrugged him off. "Our beloved King is conspiring with the King of Emperia to further Kandy's hold on the world."

"Hold on the world?"

Deux nodded. "King Kandy is hell-bent on collecting all the crystals scattered around the world even if it means stealing them from other nations. You see, he wants the entire world to bow down to him and instead of our King trying to make Kandy bow to *him* in return, he wants to help the man take over the world."

"And that's why you hate him," said Camryn in more of a statement than a question.

Deux didn't appreciate her tone. "Do not patronize me. And do not forget who the prisoner here is."

Before Deux could twist the dagger anymore, someone else walked down the stairs at the entrance of the dungeon, their footsteps echoing through the dark area. "Now is that any way to speak to a lady?" The person that spoke was a lady dressed elegantly in red who spoke with a flirtatious tone. She was clearly the seductrix known as Lilyn the Dreaded.

While Oltore remained cool as ever, Deux's tone changed when she walked, now a little more agitated. "Well, it's good of you to finally arrive, Lilyn."

"Why, did you miss me?" Lilyn's attractive smile told a story. One that suggested that she commanded any room she was in, even one with archvyrens just like her. It was clear that she didn't let anything get to her. She couldn't be insulted.

"You were supposed to lure that arker from Tandem Solaris to us. Where is he?"

"Almost here. And what have you been up to?" Lilyn sustained her smile all through the conversation.

This time, it was Oltore that answered. "Oh nothing. Deux has just been explaining every detail of our plan to our prisoner, that's all."

Lilyn didn't bat an eye. "Well as long as she ends up dead, I don't see a problem." Lilyn ignored Oltore's rolling eyes and Deux's satisfied vindication and looked at Camryn. This was the first time that she'd laid eyes on her. "So, you're the arker that's been right under our noses this whole time." A statement, not a question. Lilyn walked up close to her so that Camryn could see how extraordinarily beautiful she was. "My name's Lilyn. You're Camryn?" No answer. Again, instead of being insulted, Lilym kept her smile. "Come on now, us girls should stick together, should we not?"

Camryn decided to play her game and answered playfully. "In that case, why don't you just take this dagger out so we can talk all civilized like?" Camryn attempted her best smile but was sure it was a worthless attempt. She was surprised when Lilyn reacted with a slight movement of her head and pulled the dagger out.

"What in lloomis are you doing, Lilyn? She'll heal! Put the dagger back in."

"Oh Deux. Has anyone ever told you that you need to relax? You see, unlike you, I have faith in my abilities as an archvyren. I know I can handle myself against her if she tries to escape. Besides, we have paintings that show her in our possession until after her friends show up, do we not? So by destiny, she won't escape."

"You're a fool," said Deux, not having a better response.

Oltore, who'd watched this series of actions occur, had simply smiled. "You'd be correct, Lilyn, except for the fact that Camryn here has suggested that we don't have all the paintings and thus don't have the whole picture."

Lilyn hadn't turned away, instead toyfully ran the dagger over Camryn's skin, testing her healing factor as if curious. "Interesting, but irrelevant in the long run."

"What makes you say that?" said Deux. Deux clearly believed that the paintings were pivotal to their plan.

"Because," said Lilyn, not turning to look at him, "I've been taking note of certain events that have been happening around the world and I think there might be something larger at work."

"Such as what?" asked Deux, clearly focused on the plan.

"What events?" asked Oltore, clearly more interested in current affairs like Lilyn.

"Well for starters," said Lilyn, opting to answer Oltore rather than Deux, "I heard that there was something of a skirmish at the Nite Pole that involved a darkwielder, a vyren, a bladeslinger and, if you can believe it, a metamorpher all in the same place. Now I don't need to explain the odds of that happening and I don't need to explain the significance of the Nite Pole in all of this."

Deux was still interested in having his question answered. "And what does this have to do with our plan? How does this mean that there's something larger at work?"

"Well, we've been looking at these paintings as prophecies but treating them like they're destiny incarnate. But the truth is that destiny doesn't live on a canvas, destiny is a living thing that has us at its mercy, not the other way around."

While Deux rolled his eyes again and Oltore stood dead still, Camryn tried hard to hide her marvel. Lilyn sounded just like an arker. Only arkers looked at destiny in that way. And while it wasn't unheard of to have a mortal follow these teachings and speak like this too, to hear these words come from a creature that was inherently evil, was disturbing.

"How very existential, Lilyn. But you didn't answer my question."

"You think we captured an arker just after that happened by mistake?"

"No," said Deux, a little too quickly, "I think we captured her because of the paintings that we found."

Lilyn continued, completely ignoring Deux. "Destiny is at work here, gentlemen. And I believe that we're in the middle of history. And I, for one, don't like that we don't have the whole picture."

Deux didn't answer this time. Instead, it was Oltore who voiced his opinion about her thoughts. "It sounds like you're doubting our plan, Lilyn? It sounds like you're looking to back out of our arrangement in the name of, what, destiny?"

"That's not what I said."

"Then what are you saying?" asked Deux. "Are we going to overthrow the Vyren King or what?"

Oltore winced from Deux's carelessness, even after it had been established that they were going to kill the arker. "Deux, could you please stop revealing our plans in front of our prisoner!"

Deux had also had enough. "Oltore, I told you that she's not leaving this dungeon alive!"

"Actually," said Camryn, finally, "there's something I think I should tell you. The trap that's currently unfolding isn't for my friends. It's for you. You see, when you caught me, what you failed to do was search my home thoroughly. Otherwise, you would have noticed that I was in possession of two paintings myself. One of these depicted my capture and subsequent torture. But the other one depicted my rescue. You see, what you don't know is that prophecies are subjective. We were taught that from a young age which is why we had High Arkers to guide us whenever we saw glimpses of the future.

"The truth is, Lilyn is right, destiny is a living thing, and it can be influenced by our actions. Those paintings are nothing but a series of single moments captured in time and the moment we see them, we can choose whether to walk down that path or create a new one. When it comes to those paintings, the only way for the events in them to come true is for you to either never see them or follow the path they show. And unfortunately for you, I chose not to follow the path where I end up dead."

"Well, that's touching," said Deux, arrogantly, "but I'm afraid, sweetheart, that you won't have much choice in the matter."

"No, I won't," said Camryn smiling, "but they will."

Everything suddenly felt like it happened at once. First there was a blurring noise as a golden pillar of light swept into the room by the entrance. While the arker that had blurred in was moving faster than a mortal's eye could see, Camryn could see Twyler perfectly as he ran into the dungeon. Unfortunately, the archvyrens – who had supernatural speed of their own – could see him too as Oltore immediately gave chase with his vyren speed.

They all soon found out that it was a trap as Twyler suddenly came to a stop in the middle of the room, allowing Oltore to catch up to him when part of the ceiling caved in just above them, barely giving Twyler enough time to roll out of the way leaving Oltore to be buried by the rubble. While Deux immediately gave chase to Twyler again, chasing him around the room at supernatural speeds, Lilyn proved herself the smartest of the three and immediately jammed the dagger back into Camryn to negate her healing, cut her down and held her in front of her like a living shield.

Two people jumped down the hole in the ceiling. The first was a man who immediately jammed his sword into the heart of Oltore who was still lying half-buried in rubble. The second was a woman who looked Solari who held a red crystal in her hand, clearly a wielder. She held her other hand up to Camryn's hostage-taker.

"Ah, ah, ah!" said Lilyn, warning her. "You twitch a finger, I snap her neck. And in her state, she's pretty much mortal."

Instead of the wielder answering, it was the man who stepped forward. "My name is Captain Jon York of His Majesty's Navy. In the name of the elected King of Emperia, I order you to let that woman go."

"Or else what?" said Lilyn, staying calm. However, when the Captain revealed what he had concealed in his hand, Lilyn finally lost her smile. It was a brown crystal.

"Or I will give this to my companion here and blow this building to ashes. While you might survive the explosion, I can assure you, you won't survive the sun blistering high above our heads."

Lilyn found herself contemplating her position. Two things concerned her right now. The first was the rare brown crystal which, in the hands of a wielder, was a powerful explosive, highly unstable. The second was that the sun, while the third most lethal thing to a vyren, was still capable of killing them, just very, very slowly and painfully. Lilyn thought about her options. "If I let her go, will you let me go?"

When the Captain hesitated to answer, it was Camryn who decided to complete the bargain. "Yes, they will."

Lilyn twisted the dagger to show that she didn't believe her. "Is that so?"

"Yes, it is," said Camryn through gritted teeth. "It is because it's in our best interest to do so. You just revealed to me that you plan to overthrow the Vyren King which is not a bad thing for us. Of course, I wouldn't insult you by saying that we won't come after you another time and settle our affairs. But that's a fight for another day. Right now, you let me go, we'll let you go." Camryn looked at the Captain to back her up on this.

He nodded. "You can go, but your friend over there is fair game," said York, referring to Deux who'd caught up to Twyler and was now in a fist fight with him.

Lilyn assessed his odds fast. "I think you mean dead meat." Lilyn then let Camryn go, dropped her to the floor with the dagger still in her heart and used her vyren speed to run away, but not before grabbing Oltore and taking him away too.

"No! Dammit," said York.

"Not to worry, Captain," said the Solari wielder. "We'll get her one day. Both of them."

"I know that, Sandy. But they took my sword!"

Camryn was barely listening to them as she used what strength she had to grab the dagger in her heart and pull it out. She'd just managed the feat when York and Sandara came over to aid her. They asked if she was alright, but Camryn was focused on Twyler who was struggling with Deux. "Give this to Twyler," she whimpered. "It's the only way to kill Deux."

York took the dagger from Camryn and handed it to Sandara. "You heard the lady, Sandy." he said, almost smiling. Sandara, with something of a smile of her own and still holding the red crystal in her other hand, used her mind to throw the dagger like it was launched out of a canon Unable to give it to Twyler in such a way that he'd catch it, Sandara had instead opted to launch it into the neck of Deux.

Twyler didn't need to be told what to do next! He pulled the bone dagger out of Deux's neck and then plunged it into his heart, killing the archvyren. Deux slumped back, momentarily stunned before doubling over and falling to the ground, his skin turning a deathly grey, finally dead. Twyler then came over to her. "Are you okay?"

Camryn struggled to smile. "I am now. Boy am I glad to see you Twyler. Been a long time."

"Yes, it has, my friend. Yes, it has."

*

A couple of days had gone past before Camryn was more herself again. Twyler had opted to let her rest before getting into business. They'd opted to hide out in Hellepoint Valley where it was quiet. Twyler had used his powers to heal her best that he could but otherwise allowed *The Light* to do the rest. It was always important for an arker to focus on *The Light* for help rather than other arkers.

When Camryn finally came to, she told them how she'd found some paintings and how she'd also learnt that the archvyrens had found some others. She told them how she believed that there were more out there and also what she learnt while she'd been captured. She'd finished off by asking for Twyler's help to find the other paintings and stop the vyrens.

"I'm sorry Camryn but I can't stay. I came here to rescue you, not to join your mission."

"But this could lead to us finally being able to go home. Why can't you stay?"

"Because I have a mission of my own."

Unlike with York and Sandara who were back at the ship, Camryn understood his mission. "Twyler, I know you want to go back to Tandem Solaris, but I think your destiny is here. That girl is going to be fine."

"How could you possibly know that?"

"Because I found two other paintings, Twyler, and it showed something I couldn't explain to you. Instead, I had to show you."

"What is in these paintings?"

"You'll know soon enough. I've sent for someone to bring them to us."

It was dark when a messenger boy rode down the alley where their hideout was and handed Camryn a large flat package. Camryn waited until the boy was away to open the package and reveal the painting. In the first painting was a man with brown hair and ocean blue eyes standing in front of a young girl who looked exactly like S'kay, protecting her. Judging from the glowing golden light around him, this man clearly was an arker except he'd never seen him before.

"Who is this?"

"I don't know but he must be one of us."

"What makes you so sure apart from the glow?"

Camryn then showed him the other painting. In this painting was the same man except that this time he was alone and judging from where he was, Twyler knew that he was what she said he was: an arker, because he'd recognize that landscape anywhere: it was Fairden.

"This is impossible."

"Or inevitable. Don't you see, Twyler? Don't you realize what this means? It means this man, this arker, is the man destined to finish what you started and protect S'kay."

"What about the second painting?"

"I believe that painting is actually the first painting. I think that painting depicted him trapped in Fairden and that it's our job to go and rescue him. Twyler, I believe he's our way home."

This was crazy, surely. But Twyler couldn't help but believe. For years now, he'd been looking out for S'kay, not knowing what lay ahead but for the first time, these paintings revealed a path. What if he wasn't meant to lead her to her destiny but rather find the arker who would? What if finding this man was what would set things right? And what if, to do that, they needed to defeat the Vyren King?

Perhaps they weren't meant to be the last of the arkers. Perhaps they were only brought to the brink of extinction to help usher in a new age. Perhaps they were only the last of a previous generation and now it was time for the next to begin. Perhaps, that age was about to begin, and destiny was doing its part to bring it all together.

If destiny was a living thing, then surely it would not have set in motion the series of events it had only to have nothing serve as an outcome? No, this was happening for a reason and it was his duty to follow this through. "Alright Camryn, count me in."

Planet of the Rings

Vol. 2

The saga continues as this ground-breaking series takes the drama to new heights. Follow Sando as he journeys across the seas in an effort to get revenge on the monster that killed his beloved while Theodora looks to not only catch her sworn enemy but escape the pursuit of the bladeslingers. Meanwhile, the political ambitions of the elected King of Emperia look to bring all the corners of the world together!

ABOUT THE AUTHOR

Bernard Bayede was born Sphu T. Kubheka in the city of Durban in the beautiful province of Kwa-Zulu Natal, South Africa. Born to Thabo and Nompumelelo, Bayede enjoys spending time with family that includes his fiancé, Juliet Mentoor and sister, Naledi as well as watching motorsport. He also has an undying love for karate and construction.

Learn more about the author at: www.kubhekastories.co.za

ALSO BY THE AUTHOR

If you enjoyed *Planet of the Rings: Vol. 1*, then you should also try out Bernard Bayede's debut book: *The Bowman's Apprentice and Other Stories*. As a collection of short stories from very different genres written under his own name, Bayede gives you something for everyone.

From the writer of "The Bowman's Apprentice"

Ignighted

By Bernard Bayede

Get ready to fuel up the gas tank

Ignighted tells the tale of Max McKay who returns to the Island Province of Azania, South Africa and quickly becomes embroiled in the action-packed underground formula-style racing. From the maker of *Monday Night Fuel* comes the untold story from the era before.